SPY GEAR

ADVE

D0644068

THE DOOMSDAY
DUST

READ ALL THE

SPY GEAR

ADVENTURES

SPY GEAR

BOOK 4

ADVENTURES

THE DOOMSDAY DUST

BY RICK BARBA

ALADDIN PAPERBACKS
New York London Toronto Sydney

ALADDIN PAPERBACKS
An imprint of Simon & Schuster Children's Publishing Division
1230 Avenue of the Americas, New York, NY 10020
Text copyright © 2006 by Wild Planet Entertainment, Inc.
Illustrations copyright © 2006 by Scott Fischer
Map of Carrolton copyright © 2006 by Eve Steccati
All rights reserved. Spy Gear and Wild Planet trademarks
are the property of Wild Planet Entertainment, Inc.
San Francisco, CA 94104
All rights reserved, including the right of reproduction
in whole or in part in any form.
ALADDIN PAPERBACKS and colophon are
trademarks of Simon & Schuster, Inc.
Designed by Chris Grassi
The text of this book was set in Weiss.
Manufactured in the United States of America
First Aladdin Paperbacks edition October 2006
2 4 6 8 10 9 7 5 3 1
Library of Congress Control Number 2006924952
ISBN-13: 978-1-4169-0890-6
ISBN-10: 1-4169-0890-0

CONTENTS

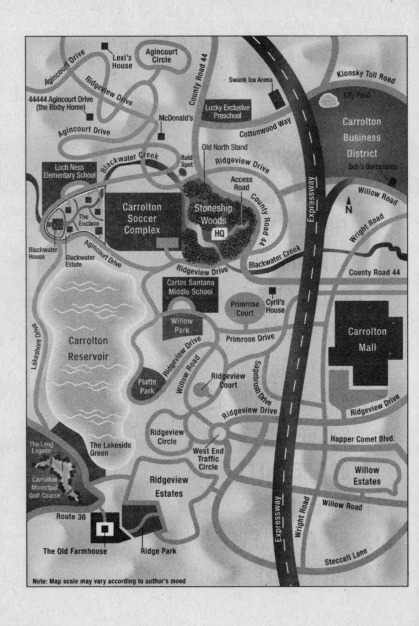

Note: Map scale may vary according to author's mood

TEAM SPY GEAR

 JAKE BIXBY

 LUCAS BIXBY

 CYRIL WONG

 LEXI LOPEZ

1

BALD SPOT

Carrolton is a great place to live, but let's be honest. In January the place is *ridiculously freaking cold*.

See it down there? It's that sleepy suburban dot in the middle of the big white region.

Zoom in on the white region.

Okay, that's snow, mostly, except for up there in Chimichanga County, which is entirely covered in baking soda. You Chimichanga kids can test this by dumping a gallon of vinegar outside. Watch the chemical reaction. Fun! This is also a good way to clean dirty coins, by the way.

But let's not lose our focus so early in the book. Rather, let's do a quick comparison. Kids, pan your satellite view south to those green areas near the equator. See them? Those are tropical forests and whatnot. It's warm there in late January—hot, even.

But Carrolton is white and cold.

Scan back north to Carrolton and then zoom in a bit more. See?

The Carrolton Reservoir is rock hard. Nearby, Blackwater Creek trickles beneath a solid glaze of ice as it snakes through the Enclave—six secluded estates belonging to Carrolton's wealthiest folks. Downtown in the business district, the City Pond is a polished diamond and teeming with ice-skaters. Everything's frozen solid. Bitter winds howl from the north, and snow covers everything.

But here's the bizarre thing:

Carrolton kids like it this way.

Because when things freeze, everything gets really slick.

By the way, *where* have you been?

Seriously, I like most of you guys, but do you really expect me to keep an eye on Carrolton all by myself? Sure, I'm the author, but I can't keep track of everything. Especially from my office up here on the International Space Station.[1]

Anyway, since you've been gone, strange things have been happening in this quiet, happy town. First, let's examine the phenomenon I've been tracking most

1. Kids, please don't tell NASA I'm here.

carefully during your absence. Please pan your satellite cameras to the south edge of Stoneship Woods. Zoom down close. Note how the northern wind rushes through the trees, scattering and twirling the dry snow. As each gust wanes, the white whirlwinds settle back into the snowscape.

Uh, except for those two.

Over there.

See them? Near the bridge where Ridgeview Drive crosses over Blackwater Creek? Right there: Two white whirlwinds, each about three feet high. Both hover above the dark creek ice . . . and continue doing so even after the wind dies.

In fact, they pulse up and down as if alive.

And now things get even more interesting.

Suddenly a long black sedan roars up Ridgeview Drive. As it passes over the creek bridge, its driver slams on the brakes. The car skids wildly, swerving sideways. The doors burst open before the vehicle even halts. Four men in black suits and dark sunglasses leap out.

Down in the creek, the two wispy whirlwinds start circling each other.

They look nervous.

One of the black-suited agents slings a heavy-looking tank onto his back as he emerges from the car. A hose runs from the tank to a suction tube that the man holds in one hand. He flicks a switch on the tube's handle and the tank suddenly whines loudly. It sounds like, well, a vacuum cleaner.

Meanwhile, the other black-suited men hop off the bridge into a snow bank along the creek. The man with the vacuum cleaner follows, fighting to keep his balance as he staggers along. Out on the ice, the white whirlwinds continue to pulse up and down, as if in confusion. The four agents approach the strange entities cautiously; they creep within twenty feet. Ten feet.

At five feet they stop. Nobody moves.

The whirlwinds seem to appraise the men for a few seconds. And vice versa.

Then the agent wearing the vacuum tank takes a slow step to the very edge of the ice. And with an abrupt, violent thrust he jabs the suction tube into the nearest of the two whirlwinds. Within seconds the white swirl disappears; its particles sucked from the air into the tank.

The other whirlwind starts pulsing wildly, almost violently. It changes colors from white to black, then back to white, then black again. It floats several feet up the creek but does not flee. Suddenly it rushes directly at the three other agents! It flows around them, over them, zooming back and forth between them. The three agents flap their hands and fan their arms at the swirling black dust, trying to drive it away. Soon, all three men are coughing violently.

The man with the vacuum tank keeps trying to aim the suction tube at the renegade entity, but the thing is lightning fast. After a few seconds, it darts back out over the frozen creek. Then, suddenly, its particles collapse, dropping straight down to form a flat black circle on the ice.

The tank-wearing agent tries to aim the suction tube at this scattering. But he's too far away. He takes a tentative step out onto the creek ice. Then another. The ice holds. One more step, and he's close enough to the whirlwind's resting place.

But as tank-man carefully extends the suction tube down toward the black circle, the entity abruptly rises again, hissing loudly—this time in a jagged, amorphous, hostile-looking shape. It flashes silver, then angry red. The agent leaps backward in fear. Crack!

For a second the man stands motionless.

Crack! Crack!

Then he falls through the ice.

The dust entity quickly reforms into a white whirlwind and escapes with stunning speed up the creek. Within mere seconds it darts around a bend.

Fortunately for the agent with the vacuum tank, Blackwater Creek is very shallow this time of year; he stands only knee-deep in the frigid water. The other three agents, still coughing, scramble toward him to help.

First things first, though:

Before they lend a hand to the fellow shivering in the creek, they demand that he hand over the tank on his back.

Okay, that's some weird, wacky stuff right there, my friends.

Now pull back and pan up to the northern edge of Stoneship Woods.

Center your focus on those really tall, old trees. That's the Old North Stand, where the last Spy Gear adventure more or less ended. Remember? If you don't, that's okay. Just grab one of your copies of *The Quantum Quandary* and reread it several times until you've got it mostly memorized. Then throw it in the trash, because you messed it up by getting fingerprints on it and whatnot. Go to the bookstore and buy a few more fresh copies with your parents' hard-earned money, knowing that it's going to a good cause.[2]

Scan farther north, just across Ridgeview Drive, then a little west toward Blackwater Creek.

See that pond next to the creek bed?

That's not a pond, actually. Rather, it's a shallow depression in the open space known as the Bald Spot. Weeks ago, somebody flooded it with creek water. Now the Bald Spot is a big ice rink.

Hey, look. Two boys are walking down Agincourt

2. Me.

Drive, which curves past the Bald Spot. They both wear big ski coats and caps. Both carry broomball sticks. Both are brothers—coincidentally, to each other. Indeed, both are named Bixby.

Let's follow them.

As these Bixby brothers step onto the ice, a skinny, thirteen-year-old kid wearing a Siberian sheepskin tundra hat with fur earflaps turns to them. He holds a plastic ball in one hand and a broomball stick in the other. Massive shoots of hair explode like black icicles from beneath his hat. The earflaps flop loosely as the lad raises his stick in salute.

"Greetings, Men of Bixby!" he intones in his deepest voice.

The Bixby boys raise their sticks in reply.

"Cyril!" Jake calls out. "Out of the doghouse, I see."

"Somewhat, yes." Cyril nods. "Mother no longer hisses or spits at the sight of me."

"That's good," says Jake as he approaches, grinning. "But I thought she grounded you because of that buried treasure thing you did with her jewelry box."

"She did." He shakes his head. "The woman has no sense of humor."

"So how is it that you're here?"

"Dude, I wouldn't miss this game for anything."

"I understand that," says Jake. "But if you're grounded, how can you . . . ?"

"I bribed her."

Jake says, "So, like, you promised to take out the trash for the next month or something?"

"No," answers Cyril. "Actually, I gave her a hundred dollars."

Jake nods. "You bought your freedom for a hundred dollars."

"That's correct, Jake."

"Because you love broomball."

"Deeply."

Lucas smirks. "But you stink at broomball."

"But I love it."

Jake gives him a sly look. "How about if I give you a hundred bucks to go home right now?"

"It's a deal!" yells Cyril.

He whips off his glove and reaches out his hand, but the two fellows laugh like jackals and undergo a complex Western greeting ritual known as a "handshake." After a handclasp, a few spins, and some knuckle punches, they flutter their fingers at each other and end it with a two-finger pointing gesture.

Cyril Wong has been Jake's best friend ever since the Jurassic era. He's quite skinny, and kind of rubbery, too. Those of you who know Cyril from previous Spy Gear adventures know about his hyperserious, scholarly demeanor. Like his mom, he has no sense of humor. It's too bad, really.

Suddenly a small dark-eyed waif wearing a purple stocking cap and a huge, blue down vest skids up next to the boys. Her long black hair flutters in the breeze.

"Avast, dogs," says the girl. She looks at Lucas and raises her stick.

"Yo, Lexter!" Lucas grins. He raises his stick too.

They clack the sticks together multiple times. Then they both bow.

Lexi Lopez, eleven, is Lucas Bixby's best friend. She's also the best gymnast in town. Plus she's made almost entirely of molecules. As a result, Lexi looks very interesting under an electron microscope. One other thing: She's the star of the broomball team.

Cyril taps the ice with his stick and turns to Lucas. "I must say, young Bixby, you've done it again, chap." He drops the ball to the rink, then rears back and whacks it violently with his stick. "The ice is perfect, my man."

"He's a mechanical genius, as you well know," Jake puts in.

"It's even better than last year's ice," calls Lexi as she scoots after the ball.

Lucas grins.

One year ago, using just a few common household items—a leaf blower, some garden hoses, two desk clamps, and a Yakmar XE 1,300-watt industrial-grade plutonium-rod power generator—Lucas Bixby managed to rig up a crude siphon pump. He used this pump to suck water from Blackwater Creek and spew it into the Bald Spot depression, flooding the central area three inches deep.

It being January in Carrolton, the water froze solid within forty-eight hours.

Once the ice was solid, Jake and Lucas put up a pair of four-by-six goals and then rounded up Cyril, Lexi, and other neighborhood kids for some broomball madness. Word spread. Soon dozens of kids with sticks were running over the ice (no skates in broomball, just shoes) every day after school, whacking at blue rubber broomballs with joyful abandon.

Indeed, attendance grew so fast that Lucas had to reassemble his siphon pump, hammer another hole in the crystal crust of Blackwater Creek, and flood the Bald Spot still deeper so the iced area grew. Kids set up a second rink. Within weeks an informal league formed. Soon the league became more formal—believe it or not, organized by kids, *with no parental involvement whatsoever*!

Of course, when Jake had first proposed such heresy, Lucas was stunned.

"But who will yell at us?" he asked. "I mean, how can we possibly hope to compete at sports without adults to belittle us into achieving excellence?"

"Good point." Jake nodded. "I don't know. I guess we'll have to play for fun."

"Fun?" scoffed Lucas. "What kind of motivation is *fun?*" He tried to blink confusion from his eyes. "I mean, how can we build character without overcoming gut-wrenching adversity? Jake, we need adult coaches to yell at us, or we aren't *learning* anything!"

Now, one year later, in deepest winter, this Bixby-created broomball arena has become the center of the Carrolton Kid World.

Today Team Spy Gear faces a tough match against the Black Dogs, a team of kids from the Willow Estates neighborhood in the south part of town. Unfortunately, our flashback to last year forced us to miss the first six minutes of the game. The score is 2–1 already, with Team Spy Gear in the lead. You also missed the three cows that ran mooing across the field, plus the Allosaurus that was chasing them. Plus the comet. You missed that, too.

Next time you read this chapter, you might want to just skip the flashback.

Anyhow, it's a pretty good game so far.

Right now Jake is playing defense. He poke-checks the ball from an attacking Black Dog, then swats it forward to Lexi. After a nifty step-over move, she slides the ball across the ice to Lucas, who is flying down the left wing. Lucas gathers the ball and holds it just long enough to draw two defensemen, then he slaps it backward to Jake, who trails the play.

Now Jake has a wide-open look from about twenty feet.

Grinning with glee, he takes a full windup and slaps a screaming missile at the goal. Unfortunately, it sails high. The goalie punches the ball higher still as it sails over him.

The ball caroms out of the rink. It skitters down a snowbank toward Blackwater Creek.

"Dang it!" yells the goalie.

"It's okay, I got it!" calls Lucas.

He scoots off the ice and tromps through calf-deep snow, then scrambles down the creek bank. The ball sits like a big blue fruit just inches from the ice. Relieved, Lucas approaches the blue sphere. But something catches his eye.

Just down the creek, maybe thirty yards away, a small flock of birds circles in a tight formation. They look like black sparrows; they circle a spot just three feet above the frozen surface of the ice.

Mesmerized, Lucas trudges a few steps closer.

The flock's circling motion is fast and follows an oddly regular pattern. Indeed, as Lucas approaches, the black birds speed up. Soon their movements are nearly a blur, so fast it seems a miracle they don't collide.

"That's so sick!" Lucas whispers in awe.

These birds are incredible! He reaches a patch of brittle, neck-high cattails jutting from the snow. As

Lucas edges forward, he uses his broomball stick to push aside reeds. When he finally emerges from the cattails, he frowns.

Up close, the birds are . . . white?

How could that be?

The flock notices him now and moves away, up the creek. Strangely, however, it continues circling near the ground. Lucas watches in wonder. When the birds near the next bend, they drop even lower. The precision of their swirling pattern is mind-boggling.

Then the birds evaporate into white dust.

Lucas blinks.

The birds are gone.

2

PACK CHALLENGE

On typical January mornings the front hall of Carlos Santana Middle School resembles the base camp of a polar expedition. This Monday, Jake and Cyril slump against a wall, watching the arrivals. Kids slog in wearing the latest high-tech cold-weather gear.

"Some of this stuff is so advanced, NASA doesn't even know about it yet," says Cyril.

"These sixth graders are soft, I tell you," Jake says, shaking his head. "We were much tougher back in our day."

Cyril stares at his buddy. "Jake, your mom used to apply latex thermo-seal to the seams of your mittens," he says.

"She did not," says Jake.

Cyril gives Jake a look.

"Well," says Jake, "okay. Maybe she did. Once." He glances at Cyril, who smiles toothily. "A day," Jake adds.

Cyril starts rearranging lumps of his hair, which his ski cap has crushed into the shape of a wild stoat. "Dude, I need to look presentable," he says. "We're meeting Cat for lunch today."

"*We're* meeting Cat?" says Jake.

"That's correct."

"What's the purpose of this meeting?" Jake asks.

"Lunch."

Jake slugs Cyril's shoulder.

"Ouch! Okay, she has another friend who wants to meet you, and—"

"*Not another one!*" yells Jake, exasperated.

Cat is Cyril's new friend, who just happens to be female. Over the past month Cat and Cyril have tried to pair up Jake with several of Cat's friends. All of these "dates" have been disastrous.

Cyril faces Jake and asks, "Be honest. How do I look?"

Jake looks at Cyril's head. "Your hair looks like a wild stoat," he answers.

"So it's good?"

"Yes."

Cyril looks pleased. "Excellent." He points at the front door. "Whoa, check out Bobby Bilkey."

A tall, redheaded boy enters the school wearing only shorts and a short-sleeved T-shirt.

"Yo, Bobby!" calls Cyril. "Little cold there, dude?"

Bobby approaches, holding up his arms. "Polypropylene wrap," he replies.

"Wow."

"It's just four microns thick," says Bobby, "but it breathes like real skin and keeps you warm down to sixty below."

Jake touches Bobby's arm. "That's . . . really sick, Bobby," he says.

Bobby frowns. "The only drawback is, I have to chew it off every night," he admits.

"Yeah," says Jake, examining the arm. "I can see scar tissue developing from the bite marks there."

Cyril chortles as Bobby moves on. "Man, it gets weirder every year, doesn't it?" He watches a small walrus waddle down the hall. "Nice tusks," he says.

The guys push off from the wall and slouch toward their first-period class: Math Difficulties with Mrs. Burnskid.

"Hey, where's your brother?" asks Cyril.

Jake points down the hall at a door that reads LIBRARY/COMPUTER LAB. "I believe he's online, using our powerful school search engine to research birds," he says.

Cyril rubs his hair, which goes *boiiing*!

"Birds?" he says.

"Yeah, birds."

"That's too bad," says Cyril.

The boys hear loud snorting behind them. They turn just in time to see Brill Joseph pull something long and elastic from his nose. Brill is the school's alpha bully. A small contingent of his followers (known as the Wolf Pack) laughs wildly as he flings the glob at a group of shrieking girls.

"Wow," says Jake, watching in morbid fascination.

"Wasn't that a tapeworm?" Cyril asks, impressed.

After a few seconds, Brill barks and leads the pack into the library/computer lab. Cyril and Jake turn away and continue down the hall.

"So is it, like, a science project?" asks Cyril. "You know, this *birds* thing you speak of?"

"No," says Jake. "Lucas is researching that flock of sparrows he saw yesterday."

Cyril starts hooting with laughter. "You mean the one that, *heh heh*, disappeared into thin air over Blackwater Creek?"

"That would be the one," Jake says with a grin.

Cyril can't restrain himself. "So he's, like, doing an Internet search on Dissolving Birds of North America?"

Jake, chortling now as well, answers, "Yeah."

Both boys cackle like jungle primates until the bell rings and Mrs. Burnskid, their gruesome math teacher, herds everyone into class with a pitchfork.

* * *

In the library, Lucas taps the Enter key on a workstation keyboard. He stares with a frown at the monitor. Then he slumps down in his chair, disappointed.

He says, "Nothing."

Lexi stands behind Lucas, looking over his shoulder. She looks slightly uncomfortable.

"Maybe it wasn't birds," she says quietly. "Maybe it was just some leaves."

Stunned, Lucas spins in his chair to look at her.

"What?" he exclaims. "You don't *believe* me?"

"Sure I do," says Lexi. "Except, you know, maybe you're wrong."

"Look, these were not *leaves*," Lucas states with earnest intensity. "These were *birds*."

"And then they just turned to dust?"

"Correct."

Lexi sees the look in his eyes. That's good enough for her. "Okay, so try a new search string," she suggests. "Try 'bird evaporation.'"

Lucas just looks at her for a second. Then he starts typing again.

Suddenly Ms. Beek, the librarian, looms over them like a condor. Both kids scream. She jabs her massive honking nose at Lucas.

"Is that a *rotting carcass* I smell, Mr. Bixby?" she asks.

(Of course, what Ms. Beek actually says is "Does this

Internet activity have anything to do with school research?" But the author put other words into Ms. Beek's mouth to really ram home the condor image.)

"Oh yes, I'm doing a science report on, like, birds and their migratory whatever," replies Lucas, flapping his hands like birds. "Like, where do they all go? So I'm doing research on the migratory patterns of, uh . . . birds." He nods enthusiastically. "We need to know where these birds go, feasibly."

Ms. Beek turns her head sideways to look at him with one eye. "A bird study?" she asks.

"Yes, because birds are so fascinating."

Ms. Beek ruffles her clothing and then turns her head the other way, studying Lucas with her other eye.

"I suppose birds are appropriate," she squawks.

Ms. Beek withdraws and returns to her nest, I mean desk.

As Lucas turns to the keyboard again, loud snickers invade the computer area. He and Lexi look up to see Brill Joseph and a few minions. Lucas tosses a nervous glance over at Ms. Beek to make sure she's at her perch, I mean post. Then he swivels to face Brill.

The bully approaches and leans down menacingly. "Hey, toad scum," he says.

"Brill." Lucas nods. He gestures at the other boys. "Been hanging around the recombinant genetics lab again, I see?"

Brill sneers. "We want a game," he says simply.

Lucas glances up at Lexi, who shrugs. "What are you talking about?" he asks Brill.

Brill gestures at his minions, then at himself. "We want a game," he says. He curls his fists around an imaginary stick, swings it at Lexi's head, and adds, "With you."

Lucas frowns. But Lexi gets it now.

"Broomball?" she asks.

"Right!" says Brill. "Wow. Pretty smart for a skaggy little girl."

Lucas bristles at this and stands up, but Lexi just laughs.

"You guys have a *broomball* team?" she asks.

"Yes, we have a *broomball* team," answers Brill, mimicking her voice.

Lucas sits back down. He grabs the arms of his chair. "Where do you play?" he asks. "I've never seen you at the Bald Spot."

Brill reacts as if smelling a bad odor. "The Bald Spot is for losers and hoodwinks!" he shouts. "We play at the Swank Ice Arena."

Lucas nods. "I see," he says.

"Well, good for you," sneers Brill.

"By the way, Brill," says Lucas, "'hoodwink' is a verb, not a noun."

"*So's your mom!*" Brill guffaws. Behind him, the Wolf Pack hacks out barking laughter.

"So let's play," says Lexi.

Lucas gapes at her. Her eyes sparkle with competitive intensity. *Wow*, he thinks proudly.

"Time and place?" Brill asks.

Lucas pulls a green notebook from the front pouch of his backpack. He flips a few pages. "Hmmm, okay . . . let's schedule for Saturday," he says. He looks up at Brill. "That would be February the second. How's nine a.m., at the Bald Spot?"

"Whatever," replies Brill. "It's your funeral."

Lucas grabs a pencil and jots in the notebook. As he does, Lexi folds her arms and steps up to Brill with a mischievous look.

"So, Brill," she begins, "what position do you play?"

Brill squints, looking confused. But then he answers, "Defenseman?"

Lexi nods. "Excellent," she says.

"Why is that excellent?" asks Brill.

"Because I'm a wing."

"So?"

"So, I'm going to nutmeg you at least twice."

For a second Brill is stunned speechless. Lucas, too, drops open his mouth in shock . . . then starts hooting with glee.

A "nutmeg," of course, is one of the most humiliating maneuvers in all of human sports. If a defender leaves his feet apart, you tap the ball between his legs and run past to gather it back, behind him. Nutmegs require skill and timing. They are more commonly seen in soccer, but they work in broomball, too.

Brill tries to respond. He splutters once or twice. Finally he blurts out, "So's your mom!"

His minions laugh again, but it sounds pretty forced this time.

Lucas looks back down at his scheduling notebook. "Uh, what's your team name?"

Brill gives him a suspicious look.

Lucas sighs. "This isn't a trick question, Brill. I just need it for the schedule."

Brill recovers a bit. He beats on his chest a couple of times. After a significant pause for effect, he growls, "We are the Wolf Pack!" Somewhere an organ blares out a scary minor chord.

Lucas and Lexi just look at him.

"Whatever," Lucas says.

"See you, pork breath," says Brill with an evil leer. Then, with a rough gesture, he orders his shaggy troops out the library door. As Brill spins to follow them, a tiny sound emits from the backpack next to Lucas's chair.

Beep!

Lucas and Lexi exchange an excited look.

Brill halts. He shoots a green-eyed glare back at them. "What's that?" he says.

Lucas's ears turn pink. "What?" he asks.

"That beep," says Brill.

"What beep?"

Beep!

"*That* beep," says Brill.

Lucas glances at Lexi and shrugs. She shrugs back and raises her hands. There is a long, unbearable pause as the Earth rotates.

Finally: "I didn't hear anything that resembles a beep or beeping, or anything," says Lucas.

"Neither did I," agrees Lexi. She looks up at the ceiling and starts whistling.

Beep!

Brill takes a step toward them. "Are you telling me you don't hear that beep?"

Lucas and Lexi listen. Time advances further and much is lost, but much is gained, also. For example, underneath the surface crust, vast slabs of near-molten rock slip into better, more comfortable positions.

"Nope," says Lucas.

Beep!

Brill stares down at the backpack on the floor. Then he points at it.

"Give me that," he says.

Lucas fights the urge to fall on the backpack and curl protectively around it, using his body as a sacrificial shield of flesh.

"Uh, *heh heh*, why?" he asks.

"Maybe because I want to see what's beeping?" yells Brill.

Lucas looks down at the backpack.

Beep!

"Say, I just heard a beep," says Lucas, stalling for time in a desperate and nearly humiliating manner. He looks back up at Lexi. "Did you hear that?"

"Hear what?" she replies.

"That beep."

Lexi listens for a few seconds.

Beep!

She looks at Lucas. "No, I didn't hear that," she says. She points at the backpack. "I didn't hear it."

Brill screams and lunges for the backpack, but Lucas snatches it at the last moment. As Brill pivots to make a menacing grab for Lucas, the younger boy tosses the pack to Lexi. Brill lunges at Lexi. She tosses the pack over his head to Lucas. Brill howls and leaps at Lucas, who flings the backpack behind his back to Lexi. Brill shrieks in bitter fury and makes a heinous swipe at the nimble girl, who dodges and flings the pack back to Lucas. And then, well, this goes on for two hours.

Just kidding.

No, actually, Ms. Beek suddenly looms like a bitter, heinous condor (I'm running out of adjectives here) and squawks, "*What* is going on here?"

Brill points fingers at both Lucas and Lexi.

24

"*They're beeping!*" he yells.

Ms. Condor stops chewing on fetid meat long enough to say, "I'll not countenance that kind of language here in My Library, Mr. Joseph."

Beep!

Everyone looks at the backpack.

Then Lexi grins. She pats Lucas. "Oh, yeah! It's a text message."

Lucas stares at Lexi. "What?"

"Your cell phone," says Lexi, nodding like a Burberry parrot with something caught in its throat.[3]

"I don't have a cell phone," Lucas says with slight irritation.

Lexi groans. "Good God," she murmurs, slapping her forehead.

Then Lucas gets it. He raises his eyebrows.

"Oh," he says. "Right. My cell phone." He laughs with just a hint of mania. "Ha! I forgot to turn it off. It must be one of those text messages from my mother, with, like, *lunch prep instructions*, you know." He nods wildly, like a Burberry parrot with something caught in its throat or gullet or whatever you call that thing a parrot swallows stuff down.

"Lunch prep instructions," repeats Ms. Beek.

Fortunately, anybody who knows Mrs. Bixby would totally accept this lie as entirely plausible.

---

3. I don't know what this looks like, actually. But you'll notice I'm really riding the bird thing hard.

"Yes," says Lucas.

Beep!

Everyone looks at the backpack . . . including the author and millions of readers anxious for this particular scene to end.

Math with Mrs. Burnskid is usually a grim, frightening experience. Rumor has it that the woman was formerly a field interrogator for the CIA in Afghanistan. Others suggest her expertise traces more directly to Stalin's forced labor camps in the Siberian gulag.

Whatever the case, today is very different. Indeed, Mrs. Burnskid's first-period Math Difficulties class has caught a merciful break.

A mandatory district "math retraining day" calls Mrs. Burnskid away shortly after she takes attendance. The substitute teacher, Mr. Sosserlick, is a small, quiet man with little round spectacles and a green bow tie. He peers down his nose at the notes of instruction left by Mrs. Burnskid and then glances nervously around the room.

"Factoring complex polynomials," he says aloud.

Several kids shriek. Outside, cattle stampede in fear.

Mr. Sosserlick blinks in alarm. "Perhaps we should turn to chapter six for some review?" he asks.

"Perhaps not!" somebody shouts from the back of the classroom.

"Well, then, let's have a study period," suggests the teacher quickly.

Cyril raises his hand and starts waving it wildly.

Mr. Sosserlick studies a seating chart, looking up at Cyril and then back at the chart several times, pointing and counting seats silently. All the while, Cyril waves his arm, bounces up and down, and makes moaning noises.

Finally, Mr. Sosserlick points at him. "Yes?"

Cyril leaps to his feet. "*Excellent idea, sir!*" he shouts. He sits back down.

Mr. Sosserlick studies the seating chart again. He looks confused. Then he glances up at Cyril and says, "Are you Priscilla Oxley?"

Cyril leaps to his feet again.

"Sir, yes sir!" he barks. He sits back down.

"Very good," says the man. He glances around the classroom with tired, timid eyes. "Study something," he implores. "Please. I beg of you."

Jake Bixby's assigned seat is by the window, and he gazes outside at the arctic scenery. It's another frigid, blustery day. This window faces north. Directly across Ridgeview Drive from the schoolyard, Stoneship Woods rises ominously, like a bunch of dark trees growing directly out of the ground.

Tapping a pencil lightly on his desk, Jake spots a small squirrel near the schoolyard fence. Then the following things happen in swift succession:

A strong wind gust blows a big plume of snow across the road.

The squirrel sits up on its haunches, eyeing the plume.

More wind separates the plume into several smaller powdery swirls.

The squirrel suddenly sprints wildly across Ridgeview Drive, heading for the woods.

Two small whirlwinds peel off from the main snow plume. They look like white dust devils, those minitornadoes of dust only a few feet high that commonly form in hot, dry weather, usually in dry fields or dusty flats.

In his mind, Jake identifies the whirlwinds as "snow devils."

The snow devils clearly travel *against* the wind now.

They follow the squirrel.

Jake drops his jaw.

The squirrel zigzags wildly. It acts as if it is being chased.

The snow devils appear to work in tandem, cutting off the squirrel's zigs and zags, seemingly *herding* it toward the tree line.

Jake drops his pencil.

The snow devils close in on the frightened animal. They engulf the squirrel just as it dives headlong into an evergreen bush.

The bush thrashes wildly for a few seconds.

Then it stops moving.

3

THE OLD MAN

In winter, Stoneship Toys Warehouse crouches in the middle of the surrounding woods like a pale fortress besieged by armies of gaunt, hungry trees. Right now, two grim sentries man the gate of the warehouse's fenced compound. One opens his backpack, pulls out a futuristic communications device known as a "walkie-talkie," and raises it to his mouth.

Hey, that's Lucas Bixby.

"Hotel Quebec calling Juliet Bravo, do you read me, over?" he says.

No response.

Lucas tries again. "Juliet Bravo, I repeat, Juliet Bravo, this is Hotel Quebec, do you read me? Over."

After another significant pause, Jake Bixby's voice

crackles from the Spy Gear receiver unit. I've got a suggestion, he says.

"Roger that, Juliet Bravo, go ahead with that suggestion, over," replies Lucas with severe professionalism.

Jake's voice says, How about we use our actual names . . . you know, instead of all this military alphabet mumbo jumbo?

Lucas stares incredulously at his walkie-talkie. It emits a crackling sound that resembles the snickering of a boy with immense hair. Lucas holds the unit back up to his mouth. "I copy that, Juliet Bravo, but be advised, I'm getting some line static."

Ah, no, that would be me, a voice snickers.

Lucas frowns. "Charlie Whiskey, is that you? Over." he asks.

Affirmative and, son, that would be MISTER Charlie Whiskey to you, says Cyril's voice. My colleague Juliet here is having some call-code issues. Right, Juliet?

There is another pause. Then Jake's voice replies, Perhaps you can see the basis for my request, Hotel Quebec.

Lexi Lopez, the other sentry at the gate with Lucas, leans over Lucas's walkie-talkie and pipes up, "I prefer real names too."

Lucas rolls his eyes. "What's wrong with you people?" he says with exasperation. "Why can't we follow standard communication protocols? Is that asking so much?"

Lexi taps Lucas on the arm.

"What?" he says, annoyed.

She says, "Jake doesn't like being called Juliet."

Yes, keen analysis of Juliet's feelings there, Lima Lima, says Cyril gravely. **I think Juliet here feels that—ow! Hey! Stop!** There follows a scuffling sound, plus much grunting. It sounds remarkably like the grappling of primitive Ice Age mammals.

"Come on, guys," Lucas pleads into his walkie-talkie. "Not now. This is an important meeting."

Aaaaaaaaggghhh! screams Cyril.

Eat snow, hairball! shouts Jake.

Oh, yeah? yells Cyril. **How about a snow pie . . . right in the kisser!**

Aaaaaaagggghhh! Jake screams.

"Well," says Lucas, turning down the unit's volume. "I guess boys will be boys."

A snowball whacks into the side of his head.

Incredulous, Lucas spins to face Lexi, who is grinning like an insane lemur as she scoops up another snowball.

Shrieking, Lucas dives.

He nails Lexi pretty good with a flying cross-body block.

Wow. Kids. They're loony.

Ten minutes later Team Spy Gear drags their battered

bodies into the abandoned warehouse. Aside from a couple of missing limbs and some internal hemorrhaging, all four kids are in excellent shape.

"Whew!" Cyril exclaims, shaking a couple of pounds of snow from his hair. "Enough tomfoolery."

"Yes," Jake says, grinning. "Let's get down to business, shall we?"

Lucas, in the lead (as usual), approaches a column of recessed slats running up the warehouse wall. He stares up at an open hatch in the ceiling.

"I really love this place," he says.

Cyril claps him on the back. "Don't we all," he agrees.

"Lead on," says Jake.

Lucas slings his backpack[4] over both shoulders and starts climbing the slats, which function as ladder rungs leading up to the hatch.

"Whirlwinds of snow, chasing squirrels," he says. "It sounds impossible, Jake."

Earlier, at lunch, Jake had reported the odd incident he'd witnessed during math class. But the raw, shrieking lunacy of Santana Middle School's lunch hour (kids surfing from table to table using plastic trays, for example) left little opportunity for in-depth discussion, so the team arranged to meet after school at their secret headquarters in Stoneship Woods. For more on

4. This backpack, as billions of kids know by now, is filled with Spy Gear gadgets, plus some unimportant clutter like homework and schoolbooks and stuff.

this abandoned warehouse facility, please refer to Books 1, 2, and 3 of the Spy Gear Adventure series. Then get a job.

Down on the floor, Cyril calls up, "Yes, impossible. It certainly lacks the plausibility of, say, birds dissolving into dust."

Jake and Cyril start snorting with laughter.

Lucas shoots a dark glance downward. Just below him, Lexi scales the rungs so easily she appears to be rising up the wall on a cushion of air.

She says, "They sound alike, kind of."

Jake, just beginning his climb, hangs from a rung and twists to look at Cyril.

"Actually," he says, "that's true."

"What do you mean?" replies Cyril.

"Well, Lucas and I both saw swirling entities," says Jake.

"Hey, that's right," calls down Lucas, who has pulled himself through the ceiling hatch. "Maybe what you saw were more bird swarms."

"No," Jake says. He narrows his eyes, trying to remember. "No, I don't think so. It was definitely just, like, white flakes swirling. And anyway, why would bird swarms hunt a squirrel?"

Cyril snaps his fingers. "By Jove, you're right!" he says. "Birds *wouldn't* hunt squirrels!"

Jake gives him a wary look.

"On the *other* hand," Cyril continues, "swirling snowflakes have *every reason* to hunt squirrels." Cyril holds up a hand. "No, hear me out on this, fellas. It's a classic battle for resources. Squirrels eat nuts, right? My guess is, swirling snowflakes eat nuts too, especially cashews. So who gets the nuts? *Only one species can prevail.* It's classic Darwinism, my friends." Cyril raises his hands and takes a deep bow. Then he looks up at Lexi, who is scrambling through the ceiling hatch. "Hey, Spunky," he calls. "Have you seen anything *swirling* lately?"

"No," she replies.

"Good," says Cyril. He starts climbing. "I'm thinking you and I should avoid these Bixby psychos until they get some therapy."

Jake grins at this. But despite the afternoon's fun and games, he's been very troubled by the odd vision of mini-cyclones acting with apparent purpose. Most unsettling of all was the poor, skittering squirrel's obvious fear of the entities.

The ceiling hatch leads up into the Stoneship control room, a high-tech communications center overlooking the warehouse floor. Team Spy Gear crosses the room to a corner, where a big console desk bristles with buttons, dials, and digital readouts arrayed beneath a bank of five video monitors.

Here's the layout:

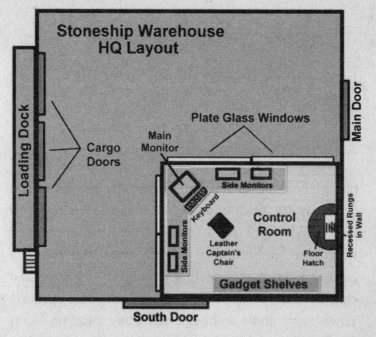

Stoneship Warehouse HQ Layout

Loading Dock

Cargo Doors

Main Monitor

Plate Glass Windows

Main Door

Side Monitors

Keyboard

Side Monitors

Control Room

Leather Captain's Chair

Floor Hatch

Recessed Rungs in Wall

Gadget Shelves

South Door

You may be wondering why we've waited until Book 4 to include this HQ diagram. We'd tell you, but the explanation is too technical.[5]

Lucas plops into the black leather captain's chair facing the huge center monitor. He slings his backpack to the floor, opens it, and pulls out a thick, leather-bound notebook. On its cover in heavy marker, it reads SPY GEAR CASEBOOK.

He opens it to a page where one word is printed in large block letters:

5. I didn't feel like it.

NANITE

"So that's the Omega Link clue?" asks Cyril.

"Yes."

"Nanite? That's *it*?"

"Yes, nanite."

What's an "Omega Link clue," you might ask? If so, put this book down. Read Spy Gear Adventures 1, 2, and 3. Take notes. You'll learn that when the Bixbys and their best friends Cyril and Lexi discovered this abandoned warehouse in Stoneship Woods, they also found a mother lode of high-tech spy gadgets—listening and communication devices, special goggles, intrusion alarms, spy robots and bugs, and other amazing secret spy equipment.

Most of these Spy Gear gadgets were easy to figure out (for Lucas anyway) and use. One, however—a simple view screen in a slim silver case—defied analysis. Dubbed the Omega Link because of the Greek omega symbol embossed on one edge, it transmits text messages that arrive with no warning other than that *beep!* you heard in Lucas's backpack back in Chapter 2.

Exactly who and where these messages are coming from is still a mystery. Some evidence suggests a source planted deep within a shadowy and perhaps rogue U.S. government intelligence outfit known only as "the

Agency." Other people think the messages come from Mars. These people are insane and must be watched.

"So what does it mean?" asks Lexi, looking at the word on the page. "Nanite?"

"No clue," Jake says.

"My guess is it's some kind of mineral," suggests Cyril. "Like bauxite or hematite. Or bixbyite."

Lucas laughs. "Bixbyite?"

Cyril flicks his eyebrows. "Don't believe me?" he asks Lucas. "Look it up. I know my rocks, dude."

Lucas poises his fingers over the console keyboard and says, "Okay, time for a power search."

Lucas types "bixbyite" into the search field and hits the Enter key. Then he clicks on the first result, which takes him to a page in a website named Minerals.com:

BIXBYITE
Type: Manganese Iron Oxide
Class: Oxides and Hydroxides
Chemical Formula: $(Mn, Fe)_2O_3$

Name Origin: American mineralogist M. Bixby Bixbyite is very rare yet well-known among mineral collectors. It forms black isometric crystals, usually cubes less than one centimeter wide. Its high luster makes it a collecting favorite.

"Ha!" Lucas laughs.

Cyril takes another bow. "They call me the Rock Man," he says. "Because I rock."

The others groan. Several readers actually throw up and swear off corn.

"Okay, now look up nanite," says Jake.

Lucas types and then clicks. The others lean over his shoulder, watching what pops up onscreen. The first few search results refer to an informational website about something called nanotechnology.

"'Nanite,'" reads Lucas. "'From nanotechnology. A nanomachine, also called a nanite or nanorobot, is a microscopic mechanical device whose size is measured in nanometers (millionths of a millimeter).'" He looks up at Jake. "That's, like, *really* small."

Jake points at an info sidebar on the screen. "Check *that* out," he says.

He reads:

In 1997 a student at Cornell University used nanotechnology to build the world's smallest guitar. Using a CAD (computer-assisted design) program, he designed the instrument on a computer; then it was etched into silicon. Each string was just one hundred atoms in diameter and could be plucked using an atomic force microscope.

"That's *sick!*" says Cyril, impressed.

"And speaking of sick, look at this," says Lucas, clicking open another window. He reads the following paragraph:

Specialized nanorobots might be designed to diagnose and treat disease conditions by seeking out invading germs and destroying them! Thus, medical nanites could enter the bloodstream and cure infections.

"Wow, that's incredible," says Jake.

"Nanites in your bloodstream," says Cyril with a shiver.

"Ugh," says Lexi.

"Exactly!" yells Cyril, pointing at her. "Sounds like really fantastic fun."

Lucas clicks through a few more pages of search results. One links to a videogame—"nanite torpedoes" are weapons in a real-time strategy game called Star Phaser VI: Battle Cauldron of Wardok IX, Part 3—The Sequel. Another link leads to a site for a corporation called Intelligent NanoSystems, or INS.

"Hey, they're based right here in Carrolton," says Lucas. "Look at the address: 3000 Lakeshore Drive."

"Where's that?" Lexi asks.

"Lakeshore runs up the west side of the reservoir," replies Lucas. "You know, where all those huge honking houses are sitting right on the waterfront?"

"Oh yeah," says Lexi, remembering.

"Huh," Jake says. "I thought Lakeshore Drive was all houses. I don't recall seeing any office buildings over there." He points at the screen. "Click on that link. The one that says 'The NanoSystems Advantage.'"

Lucas clicks to open up another window listing "the many advantages of nanosystem solutions," including the following:

- **Nanites require only a tiny amount of energy to operate and are very durable; indeed, nanite swarms might last for centuries before degrading.**
- **Nanite systems can be programmed to self-replicate by seeking carbon-based raw materials, then breaking them down into the basic components necessary to construct new nanites.**

"Carbon-based raw materials?" Cyril chuckles. "Uh, isn't that basically what I am?"

"Well, not your hair," says Lexi.

Both Bixbys point at her and start whooping.

"Oh, *zing!*"

"You served him, dude!"

"He's *down!* He's *out!* Good *night!*"

"What *now?* What *now?*"

Lexi grins and raises her arms in triumph.

Cyril smiles viciously but nods. "Okay, score one for Spunky," he says.

Suddenly, a robotic voice blares from speakers in a small metal case marked SPY TRACKER SYSTEM sitting on the console: *"Sensor 1! Sensor 1! Sensor 1!"*

All eyes turn to the case.

"Sensor one?" says Lucas. "That's the west perimeter."

"Quick!" says Cyril. "Activate the west minicam views."

Lucas slaps at a button and the two right-side monitors flicker to life over the console. Then he clacks a few keys on the keyboard. Two live camera feeds pop onto the flickering screens.

"There he is!" shouts Cyril, pointing at one monitor.

On the screen, an elderly man staggers through snow along the perimeter fence on the west side of the warehouse yard. Behind him, Blackwater Creek sits in glacial silence. Strangely, the old man wears no coat or hat, despite the frigid temperatures. And he seems to be talking to himself with creepy vigor.

"Good gosh," says Jake, staring.

Lexi looks worried. "Is he lost?" she asks. "Maybe he's in trouble."

"Let's get a close-up," says Lucas.

Using the mouse, he centers the camera on the old man. Then he clicks an onscreen zoom button. As the view zooms closer, the old man turns his back to the camera. He gazes upward at treetops. He gestures wildly, as if yelling at the woods.

"Who is that guy?" asks Cyril.

The others shrug or shake their heads.

Jake says, "Never seen him before."

"Interesting," says Lucas, frowning. "It appears our redundant alarm systems failed."

Jake looks at his brother. "What do you mean?"

Lucas clicks and holds, then drags the screen to the right. "There," he says. "That's where he tripped the Spy Tracker pod. We planted Sensor One there, in that juniper bush."

"I remember that," says Jake.

"But I also laid out Lazer Tripwire grids at each corner of the compound, including southwest, here, and north-west, here," says Lucas, moving the camera farther right, then panning left past the old man. He shakes his head. "He couldn't have reached the Spy Tracker pod sensor without tripping one of those laser alarms, too."

Suddenly the old man turns and looks directly into the camera. Even though it couldn't be so, it seems as if he's staring through the monitor, directly at the kids. Then his mouth starts moving again. Chills go up Jake's spine.

"Is he talking to us?" asks Lexi nervously.

"No way," says Lucas. "The Minicam is tiny and well hidden. He couldn't know it's there."

"What's up with his eyes?" asks Cyril.

Lucas leans closer to the monitor. "I don't know," he says. "They look messed up."

"They look kind of . . . milky," says Lexi, leaning in closer too.

All of a sudden, the old man twitches violently. Reflexively, the two younger kids jerk back from the screen. Then the man spins. He turns in a complete circle once, twice, three times, four times—a quick, tight spin.

"What the monkey is he doing?" Jake asks.

Looking disoriented, the old man stops spinning. He seems to shout something toward the camera. Then a frightened look comes over his face. He turns abruptly and stumbles awkwardly through a snowdrift toward the tree line to the north. It's apparent that he's now in a hurry to escape.

"There he goes!" says Jake.

"He's on the run!" says Lucas.

Concerned, Lexi leans toward the monitor again. She says, "He's sick."

Lucas nods grimly. "Maybe. But in any case, he now knows about our secret warehouse."

Instinctively, Jake pushes away from the console, heading for the floor hatch.

"Let's go!" he says.

STRANGE TRACKS

Roll cameras! Action!

Team Spy Gear bursts from the warehouse. The kids sprint east through the entry gate, pivot right, and leap over snowdrifts outside the security fence. Jake leads the pack around the fence line. Tense music is pounding. In fact, could you turn it down just a bit? I really can't concentrate.

When Jake reaches the west perimeter, he skids to a halt and points at the ground.

"Footprints!" he cries.

"The game is afoot!" shouts Cyril. He looks at Jake. "Lead on, Custer."

Jake dashes ahead. The footprints lead north into the trees. This is unfortunate, of course. Spring to fall, Stoneship Woods is alive with buzzing menace. But in winter, the place is even worse—a ghastly boneyard, eerie and pale. Trees moan and slash with their skeleton fingers as you pass.

Cyril trips over a nasty root. "Aaaaagghh!"

Jake and Lucas turn back and yank Cyril to his feet.

"Come on, he's getting away," says Jake.

Lucas peers up ahead. "He can't be far," he pants. He pulls a Micro Agent Listener from his coat pocket, turns it on, and hooks the earpiece on his ear. "Let's see if he's nearby."

Lucas aims the extendable mike at the trees up ahead. Amplified forest sounds mingle with his own breathing, heavy from running. Then he hears it—a low rustling, some branches cracking, and the unmistakable murmur of a human voice.

"Got him marked," says Lucas excitedly. "The poor guy's still talking to himself."

"Despicable old coot," grumbles Cyril as he starts running again.

"He's not despicable," says Lexi.

"How do you know?" Cyril says. "Maybe he's the guy who invented chives."

Lexi gives him a look.

"Never mind," gasps Cyril. He grabs his hair, trying to hold it in place as he runs.

Jake sprints out into the lead again. He cuts around a scotch pine and, once again, skids to a halt.

He stares down at the ground.

Then he looks left and right.

"The tracks stop here," he says, confused.

"What?" exclaims Lucas, who rushes up next to his brother.

Sure enough, the trail stops at a wall of twisted chokecherry trees. The old man's footprints circle in a tight loop several times. But no tracks lead away from this ring of disturbed snow.

"Peculiar," says Cyril as he and Lexi join the Bixby brothers.

Jake moves left, pushing his gloved fist into the spiky, almost serrated branches, probing for a way through. Nothing! Now he moves right, punching and poking. Again, no luck. He returns to the circle of footprints.

"This is barking madness," Cyril states, eyeing the hostile chokecherry claws.

"How did he get through?" wonders Jake.

"Maybe he crawled," Lucas says, peering low.

"I could get through, no problem," says Lexi.

"We know *that*!" says Cyril. "But what about a normal human being?"

"Okay, okay," says Jake, gritting his teeth. He takes a deep breath. "Okay."

"What does 'okay' mean?" Cyril asks. "What are you doing?" He grabs Jake's arm. "Get that look of gritty determination off your face."

Jake nods and says, "Follow me."

"Where?"

"I'm going in."

"No!"

"Yes."

Shielding his eyes, Jake lowers a shoulder and crashes into the chokecherry jungle. Tree talons rake at his face. Dry, frozen limbs crack and splinter as he staggers forward. For a few seconds he feels lost, swallowed. But Jake keeps surging forward and finally emerges into a small clearing. Flailing with momentum, Jake tumbles face-first into the snow.

Pushing himself up, he sees tracks.

"Here it is!" he shouts. "The trail starts again, right here!"

Behind him, Lucas and Lexi suddenly spew out of the tangle.

"Sick!" says Lexi, grinning.

"That was disgusting," says Lucas, wiping tree saliva off his parka.

Jake glances behind them. "Where's Cyril?"

They hear a scream from the trees.

Jake rolls his eyes. He stands up.

"I'll get him," he says.

Jake pushes a few feet into the brush to find Cyril curled up in a fetal ball.

"Are you okay?" asks Jake.

"No."

"What's wrong?"

Quietly, Cyril replies, "I've lost the will to live."

"Come on, the old dude's getting away."

Cyril sighs loudly. Then he says, "All right."

The two boys emerge from the trees to find Lucas examining the footprints. He points and says, "Look how far they start from the trees."

Nearby, Lexi marches a good ten steps from the tree line to the place where the tracks start again. "He jumped, like, insanely far," she says.

Cyril looks uneasy. "Maybe he pole-vaulted over."

Jake feels a sudden twinge of alarm. Something doesn't add up.

"This is . . . very odd," he says slowly.

Lucas starts running through the snow, following the tracks. "Come on!" he cries. "Let's find this guy."

"Let's be careful, though!" calls Jake.

"Hey, he's old," Lucas shouts, stumbling ahead. "How dangerous could he be? Come on!"

Jake hesitates a second, then starts after his brother. Cyril and Lexi follow.

Behind them, a dark figure watches for a second. Then it follows too.

It moves with power and stealth, and its red eyes lock onto Cyril's back.

* * *

Not far away, just north of the woods, a blue Toyota Avalon with brand-new snow tires crunches over the packed snow on Ridgeview Drive.

The driver is Mr. Latimer. He's lost.

But, as all Spy Gear Adventure fans know, this isn't disturbing news.

You see, Mr. Latimer has been lost in the Bixbys' neighborhood for three years, ever since taking the Carrolton exit from the expressway in search of coffee. Since then, nobody has yet managed to direct him back onto the expressway.

Things have worked out well, though. Mr. Latimer has become a sort of neighborhood watchdog. He keeps an eye on things. In exchange, folks feed him. He gets invited to a lot of birthday parties.

Everybody likes Mr. Latimer. Parents, kids, dogs—everybody.

Today he cruises past Stoneship Woods, listening to Mozart's Sonata in D Major. His car is warm, the music is good, and he's happy. As he crosses over Blackwater Creek, he catches a glimpse of squirrels hopping up the creek bank—maybe six squirrels in all.

Mr. Latimer slows the car to watch them. He's never seen so many squirrels in one spot. He smiles because he's learned to love nature. He has a lot of time on his hands, and he spends much of it watching things.

But then the smile turns to a frown.

Something is very odd about these squirrels.

Mr. Latimer turns left on Agincourt Drive, following the squirrel six-pack as it hops due west toward Loch Ness Elementary School.

The old man's footprint trail veers west to Blackwater Creek. Then it turns sharply north and continues along the creek bank.

Up ahead, Lucas halts.

"It stops again," he says, huffing vapor.

The others catch up. Jake examines the ground. Sure enough, the footprints run through the middle of a flat, open stretch. Then the trail ends in a swirling circle of disturbed snow.

"Looks like he was confused," says Lucas, "going in circles, and then . . . huh." He looks upward.

"Geez," Lexi says. She looks up at the sky too. "Did he fly away?"

Cyril and Jake exchange a glance.

"Wait!" cries Lucas. "It starts again . . . down there." He points toward the creek, where two long, deep footprints, side by side, gouge the snow. "It looks like a landing and then . . . a skid." He scans ahead. "Then he starts running again."

"I don't like this," says Jake.

"Agreed," Cyril says.

There is a silence as Team Spy Gear contemplates the

weirdness. Then, in a wordless instant, a group decision is made.

Three kids plunge ahead.

Cyril sighs and follows. But then he hears a muffled snort behind him. He spins to face the sound.

Nothing there.

He scans the nearby trees. "Hello?" he calls.

Nothing. No movement. No sound.

Cyril backs up a few steps, then turns and sprints after the others.

The footprint trail continues north along the bank of Blackwater Creek. Along the way, the odd spacing continues. The tracks lengthen, shorten, circle occasionally, and sometimes disappear for several feet, as if huge leaps were made.

"Hey, wait up!" Cyril gasps, finally catching up.

"We're almost out of the woods," calls Jake over his shoulder.

"Very funny," says Cyril.

"No, I'm serious."

The tracks finally emerge from Stoneship Woods and dip under the Ridgeview Drive overpass. They continue past the Bald Spot ice rinks and then follow the creek beneath two more overpasses.

"Oh, look, up ahead!" shouts Cyril. "It's *Canada!*"

Jake grins. "Actually, I think we're heading west now, toward Loch Ness."

Mr. Latimer eyes the squirrel pack as it hops toward Loch Ness Elementary School.

And here's the odd thing: *All six squirrels hop in perfect unison.*

To Mr. Latimer, it seems like he's watching the same squirrel, multiplied by six. Every few hops, the squirrels stop, sniff, and peer around cautiously. But they do *this* in perfect unison too.

After a few more hops, the squirrels dash into a bush near the front entrance of the school.

"Hmmm," says Mr. Latimer.

School is out for the day, of course, so Mr. Latimer pulls his Toyota into the drop-off circle by the front entrance. He keeps a sharp eye on the bush. In the nearby school yard, kids toss snowballs and climb on the monkey bars. Then two boys wearing bright orange crossing-guard vests push through the front door of the school building. They approach the school flagpole, unravel its rope, and start lowering the flags for the night.

Mr. Latimer rolls down his window and calls out, "Hey there, Martin!"

One of the boys, Martin Bell, waves. "Hello, Mr. Latimer." He whacks the other boy on the arm. "Yo, Trevor! Say hello to Mr. Latimer, dog brain."

The other boy, Trevor Murch, whacks Martin. "You're the dog brain."

"No, I think you are."

"Maybe I should *bark* so you understand me."

"Maybe your mom barks."

"Maybe you're a dork."

As the two stooges slap at each other, laughing like lunatics, the wind whips up. A few puffs of dry snow swirl past. Then a white foggy mist curls out of the hedge where the squirrels are hiding.

Mr. Latimer watches the fog float lazily toward the boys.

As it approaches them from behind, the mist thickens. Now it's swirling, milky, almost liquid. Then, slowly, it gathers itself into a hostile shape.

Eyes big, Mr. Latimer rams his stick shift into first gear. Yanking the wheel, he stomps his foot on the accelerator. Tires howl as the Toyota slams over the curb and swerves toward the boys.

Then Mr. Latimer lays on the horn.

The piercing blare scares the holy living catfish out of Martin and Trevor. Both see Mr. Latimer's car approach; both shriek and dive to the side. Behind them, the fluid fog recoils and breaks up. The milky mist swirls apart into smaller whirlwinds that abruptly whisk away in different directions.

Shaken, Mr. Latimer leans out his window. "You boys okay?" he calls out.

Neither boy can speak.

"Sorry, guys," says Mr. Latimer, struggling to keep his voice steady. "I just . . . my foot slipped."

There is a moment of silence. But this is shattered by the full-throttle roar of a car engine down the street. Skidding wildly, a black BMW pulls away from the curb and fishtails down icy Agincourt Drive.

Mr. Latimer grips his steering wheel tightly.

That car again, he thinks.

As Mr. Latimer watches the BMW disappear around the corner, an elderly man suddenly lurches past on the sidewalk. Mr. Latimer turns to glance at the old fellow.

Then his mouth drops open.

He says, "Dan?"

"Ah, civilization," says Cyril, wincing at the sounds of a car horn and screeching tires.

"Is there, like, a Grand Prix auto race scheduled for today?" asks Lucas, listening to the racket.

Jake grins. "Maybe," he says.

The team scrambles up a steep bank from the creek bed onto Agincourt Drive. The footprint trail merges onto the shoveled and salted sidewalk that runs past Loch Ness Elementary . . . and thus the tracks disappear.

"Crud!" says Lucas. "After all this, we lose him."

But suddenly Lexi bursts into a full sprint down the sidewalk past the school.

"There he is!" she calls, hair flying.

Sure enough, the old man stands fifty yards down Agincourt Drive. He stares up at a tall stone wall inlaid with squares of elegant iron grillwork. This wall runs the entire length of the street opposite the Loch Ness school yard. It marks the tasteful but forbidding boundary of the most exclusive neighborhood in Carrolton: the Enclave.

"Hey!" cries Lexi. "Hey, mister!"

The old man whips his head toward her. Then he spins around again—one, two, three times—and abruptly lurches down the street. His movement is jerky, unsteady. But he moves with surprising speed for an old man. In seconds he disappears around a corner.

As the boys rush after Lexi, Jake notices the blue Toyota Avalon idling in the drop-off circle in front of Loch Ness Elementary. He gives a quick wave to the driver, who waves back.

The kids make a beeline for the spot where the old man disappeared. Just around the corner, Agincourt Drive passes over Blackwater Creek yet again. But fresh footprints veer down to the creek bank, running along the stone wall; then the tracks cut straight across the frozen stream. Here the creek flows through a cement spillway blocked by an iron grate. Thus Blackwater Creek exits the Enclave, but nothing may enter here.

"Rich people are so paranoid," Lucas says, gazing up at the stone wall.

"They think poor people want to jack their stuff," adds Lexi.

"Well, they probably worked hard for it," says Lucas.

"Maybe they didn't," says Lexi. "Maybe they inherited it, or stole it."

"So what?"

"So, it isn't fair," Lexi says.

"Nothing's fair," says Lucas.

Lexi looks angry. "That's a lame attitude."

Cyril steps between them. "This is no time for politics," he says. He glances apprehensively at the spillway, then over at Jake. "Captain, do we dare cross this deathtrap?"

Lucas looks up the creek bank. "We could just go back up to the road, cross over the bridge, and come down the other side."

"Not necessary," says Jake. "Here, I've got an idea."

He steps gingerly onto the creek ice. It holds. Then he grabs the iron grate and pulls his weight upward to minimize pressure on the ice surface. Moving slowly, he slides and pulls himself across the spillway.

Halfway across, Jake catches a glimpse of movement through the grate: About fifty yards upstream, a dark figure pushes through a row of hedges surrounding a gloomy stone mansion. This massive house spans Blackwater Creek. It looks like a cross between a castle and a medieval stone bridge. The stream flows beneath it, through a majestic stone arch. In the dusk, most of its windows glow with pale yellow light.

Wow, Jake thinks. *That's an awesome house.* Then he calls back to the others, "He's heading for that big mansion."

Now the others follow Jake's lead, using the same technique—with no mishaps, although Cyril moans loudly as he goes last. When he sees the stone mansion through the iron grate, he gasps, "Blackwater House!"

Jake says, "You know that place?"

Cyril hangs from the grate, staring upstream. "And I thought it was just a myth." Then he notices movement to the south. "Hey, something's coming."

Jake scoots onto the ice and grabs the grate again over the spillway. The two older boys cling and watch as two long white limousines crunch slowly up the estate's driveway. The cars stop at a staircase leading up to the mansion's south entrance. Shaggy pine trees block much of the view, but Jake can see doors swing open on one car. Several men in light gray trench coats and matching hats emerge and stand by the vehicle.

Then someone emerges from the mansion door.

The glimpse is quick, but chilling. A very tall, hooded figure draped in a light gray cloak descends the stairs. He moves fluidly enough, but something about his stature is unnatural. He stoops badly, leaning so far forward it almost appears as if a second, smaller figure trails under the cloak.

Jake and Cyril exchange a startled look.

In a fleeting second, the figure disappears behind trees.

The gray-coated men reoccupy the limo. Its doors slam shut. Then both white cars round a loop in the drive and exit the estate. From his position, Jake cannot see the cars pull out onto Agincourt Drive, but he hears them roar away to the east.

"What was that?" asks Cyril.

Jake just shakes his head. "Let's see where the old man's tracks lead us," he says.

The boys rejoin Lucas and Lexi. On the far side, Jake leads the team up the bank, following the old man's tracks along the stone wall. The footprints run a few more yards until they turn sharply left—directly into the wall.

There, they disappear.

Jake places his hands on the stonework. He feels around, looking for some kind of entrance. "This is solid rock," he says. He stares at the wall face. "How'd he get through?"

"Maybe he went over," says Lucas.

"But it's smooth."

Lucas just shrugs and shakes his head.

"You know what's on the other side, don't you?" says Cyril in a hushed voice.

The Bixbys and Lexi turn to Cyril.

"No, what?" asks Jake.

Cyril gazes wide-eyed at the wall. Then he points at it and says, "That's Blackwater House."

"So?"

Cyril is stunned. "You've never heard of Blackwater House?"

"No. Should I have?"

Cyril chuckles bleakly, like a man gazing at his own gravestone.

Suddenly a car horn sounds. The kids jump in alarm.

"Whoa, it's Mr. Latimer," says Cyril with relief. He plods out to the street, where the blue Toyota Avalon idles. The passengerside window drops.

"How are you, Cyril?" says Mr. Latimer.

Cyril bangs his gloves together. "I'm essentially numb, Mr. Latimer," he says. "My head aches. My tongue feels swollen and painful." He nods. "But thanks so much for asking, sir."

"Hop in," says Mr. Latimer. "I'll blast the heater and give you all a lift home."

"Thanks!" Jake calls as he approaches.

Team Spy Gear piles into the car and fastens seat belts as Mr. Latimer cranks up the heat. Jake, in the front passenger seat, turns to the driver.

"Mr. Latimer, do you know anything about Blackwater Estate or that big mansion in there?" he asks.

"Pretty spectacular, isn't it?" says Mr. Latimer.

"Yes, it's amazing."

"I've only heard vague rumors and such," Mr. Latimer tells them. "Ghost stories, mostly."

Jake nods with interest. "Like what?"

Mr. Latimer shakes his head. "It was built back in the 1920s," he says. "Actually, if you want to hear Blackwater stories, you should stop by the old barbershop downtown. A lot of old-timers hang out there, and Bob the Barber knows everything about old Carrolton." He glances up the street, looking distracted and a little uneasy.

Jake notices the uneasiness. "Is something wrong, Mr. Latimer?"

"Well, Jake, actually, I just saw Old Dan Dunnagin run down the street," he says.

"You saw that old guy?"

"Yes, I saw him."

"And you know him?" asks Jake.

"Not really," Mr. Latimer replies. "I met him only once, about a year ago." He frowns. "Unforgettable fellow, though."

"Why don't *we* know him?" asks Lucas.

"He's a recluse."

Jake says, "Well, we've been following him through the woods."

Mr. Latimer looks bewildered. "The woods?"

Lucas leans forward from the backseat. "Mr. Latimer, did you notice him, like, spin around a bunch or mumble or, you know, act *strange* at all?"

Mr. Latimer gives Lucas a concerned look. Then he says, "Strange? Yes. Old Dan was acting *very* strange."

"How so?" Jake asks.

"Well," says Mr. Latimer, "he ran down the street."

The Bixby boys just stare at him, waiting. Mr. Latimer shrugs.

"So . . . that's strange?" asks Jake.

"Yes, it's strange," says Mr. Latimer.

Jake smiles wryly. "Why, sir?"

Mr. Latimer puts his car in gear, pulls away from the curb in a quick U-turn, and starts driving down Agincourt Drive in the direction of Cyril's house.

He says, "Old Dan Dunnagin has been blind for thirty years."

5

TALES OF BLACKWATER HOUSE

During lunch the next day, Jake sits nervously across the table from Cyril's new friend, Cat Horton. Next to Jake, Cyril hunches over a meat loaf sandwich, masticating loudly. Cat watches this brutal devouring of meat with sick fascination.

"Gosh, that sounds tasty," Cat comments.

"Verily, it's fine meat," says Cyril. He swallows a hunk and turns to Jake. "Can I see your algebra notebook, dude?"

"*What?*" Jake asks.

"Your math notebook," says Cyril. "Let me see it."

Jake pulls a spiral notebook from his backpack and hands it to Cyril. Cyril opens it, rips out a blank sheet of paper, and wipes his mouth with it.

"Thanks," he says.

Cat watches this with a thin smile. Then she says, "I love our lunches together."

"Me too," Cyril says. "It's like Paris in spring, only louder and more frightening." He rips open a bag of chips. "Dang, I love chips. Without them, I just wouldn't have enough maltodextrin in my diet."

Jake snickers, but Cat just stares at Cyril as if studying a rare beast. Jake quickly assesses her, which he's avoided doing thus far for fear of making eye contact. Cat's face is round and smart, with dark eyes glittering behind narrow, black-rimmed eyeglasses. Her dark brown hair is dyed with a henna tint today.

"So Cat is short for Catherine?" Jake asks.

"Yes," says Cat.

"What?" exclaims Cyril. "You told me it was short for Emily."

"That was a joke," says Cat, stealing a chip from Cyril's bag.

"So I can call you Catherine if I want?" Cyril asks.

"Sure," says Cat. "But then I'd follow you home and chop up your mailbox with a hatchet."

Cyril stares at her with his mouth hanging open.

Cat quickly looks at Jake, catching him gazing at her. Completely off guard, he blurts out the foremost thing on his mind: "Hey, you're a figure skater!"

She regards him warily. "Hey, I am," she says.

Jake nods. "That's good, or whatever." He clears his throat. "This skating activity." There is a pause. Then he continues, "Do you like it?"

Cat gives him a dark look. "I've been skating since I was three," she says. "I don't really know if I like it."

Jake nods, understanding. He says, "Wow."

Cat narrows her eyes. "Why, Bixby? Are you some kind of ice-skating freak?"

"No, I *hate* ice-skating," he says loudly.

In the silence that follows, everybody within a twelve-hundred-yard radius stops what they're doing and stares at Jake. Mortified, he tries to recover by acting bored.

"Yeah," he says. "So. *Hooooo* boy." He sighs and shoots a sideways glance at Cyril, who looks extremely amused. "I like broomball," says Jake. "No skates. Just run around, whack a ball with a stick." He shrugs. "Kill people."

Cat almost smiles. "Fun," she says. "Was it invented by swarthy Vikings?"

"It's uncivilized," Jake admits. He can't help it; now he unleashes one of his famous grins. "Which leads to my point, such as it is," he continues. "You train at the Swank Ice Arena, right?"

"Right," says Cat.

"It's a private facility."

"Correct."

"But you have a membership," says Jake.

"I do," says Cat.

Jake quickly explains about the impending broomball match with Brill's team.

"Whoa, let me get this straight," Cat says. She looks at Cyril. "You guys are playing the Wolf Pack."

"Yes," says Cyril.

"In a sport," Cat goes on, "where everybody is armed with sticks."

"That's right."

Cat reaches across the table and pats Cyril on the shoulder. "Hon, I've got *plants* with more intelligence than that," she says.

"Nobody said it was intelligent," says Cyril testily.

"But it's über-manly." Jake grins. "Anyway, as I understand it, Brill and his boys practice at Swank." He looks at Cat again. "It sure would be great if we could get a peek at their tactics and skills."

Cat gives him a perplexed look. "You want a *scouting* report?" she asks. "Guys, I don't know the first thing about broombat."

"That's broom*ball*," corrects Cyril.

"Exactly," says Cat. "I wouldn't know what to look for."

Jake grins again. "The only thing you'd have to look for," he tells her, "is a dark, deserted corner."

Cat thinks about this for a moment.

Then she says, "Well . . . actually, I'm pretty good at stuff like that."

* * *

Team Spy Gear's after-school tasks require a split into two units, designated Go Team One and Go Team Two.

Go Team One consists of Cyril and Lucas, who accompany Cat to Swank Ice Arena for deployment of certain high-level reconnaissance devices.

Go Team Two is Jake and Lexi, who head directly downtown to Bob's Barbershop. As per Mr. Latimer's advice, Jake plans to chat with Bob about Blackwater House.

Go Team One

Lucas looks stricken with doubt as he hands a small rucksack to Cat just outside the entrance to Swank Ice Arena. "Please," he says. "Be careful with this. I beg of you."

"Chill," says Cat.

Cyril throws an arm around Lucas.

"Honey, this is Lucas Bixby," he says. "He *cannot* chill."

Cat rolls her eyes. "It's just a little car."

"No," says Lucas desperately. "No. It is *not* just a little car."

Cyril intercedes again.

"I'm *sure* she understands," he says to Lucas. "Dude, you've thoroughly explained everything in excruciating technical detail. Now you must let go." He gives Lucas a shake. "Let go!"

Lucas relaxes his shoulders a bit.

"Go now," says Cyril to Cat. He glances at Lucas and adds, "Go quickly."

"Wait!" says Lucas.

Cyril sighs.

Lucas looks at Cat. "You'll need this, too," he says.

He hands her a Spy Link headset and base unit, then shows her how to put it on. He and Cyril don their own Spy Link sets.

"Testing, one, two, three," says Lucas.

"Roger wilco,"[6] says Cat in a manly voice. "I'm going in, Sarge."

Cyril grins as Cat snickers and enters the arena. Then he suddenly sneezes, twice.

"You don't sound too good," Lucas says.

Cyril nods. "I'm coming down with something." Then he blasts a monster sneeze. "Whew! Call 911."

You just blew out my eardrum, you donkey, says Cat over the Spy Link.

Go Team Two

Jake and Lexi stare up at the spiraling red, white, and blue stripes of an old-fashioned barber pole. It spins silently above the entrance to Bob's Barbershop on Main Street in the Carrolton business district.

Suddenly the shop door bursts open.

6. "Roger wilco" is an old Navy abbreviation. "Roger" indicates the letter R which stands for "received," as in "message received." "Wilco" is a military abbreviation for "will comply."

"Young Mister Bixby," booms a deep voice.

A huge man with a full gray beard and mustache steps out onto the sidewalk. He folds huge, hamlike arms across the front of his white smock.

"Time for a haircut," says the man. "Getting shaggy there, boy."

Jake, of course, has insanely short hair. He grins up at Bob the Barber.

"Bob, this is Lexi," says Jake, pointing at his Go Team partner. "She's a girl."

"Hmmm," says Bob. He leans down and looks at Lexi. "We'll trim your sideburns extra short, then."

Lexi giggles.

"Come on in," Bob booms. "It's cold as a freezer burn out here."

Jake and Lexi follow Bob into the shop. One customer, a large fellow, sits tilted way back in one of the shop's two barber chairs. His face is wrapped in a hot towel, a standard preshave treatment. The only other occupant is an elderly gentleman sitting in a corner, reading a fishing magazine.

"Slow day," says Jake.

"Yes, well, folks tend to hang on to their hair when it's cold," says Bob. He taps the shoulder of the man wrapped in the hot towel and says, "How you doing, bub?" The man raises a thumb in response. Then Bob swivels his other barber chair around. "Hop up, Jake."

"Actually, I'm not here for barbering today," says Jake. "We wanted to ask you some historical questions about Carrolton."

Bob looks pleased. He rests his massive hands on the back of the barber chair. "Is this something for school?" he asks.

"Uh, no," Jake replies. "We're just curious about that big old stone mansion that runs over Blackwater Creek in the Enclave."

Now Bob doesn't look so pleased.

"Blackwater House," he says, frowning. "Hmmm."

Bob shoots a quick glance over at the old fellow in the corner, who has lowered his magazine to scrutinize the kids.

"What can you tell us?" asks Jake.

"Well," says Bob. "Horace Jasper probably knows more about Carrolton's past than anybody in town."

"Who's Horace Jasper?" Lexi asks.

"*I'm* Horace Jasper," rasps the old man in the corner. His voice sounds like somebody strangling a Burberry parrot. He leans forward and glares at Lexi. One eye is considerably bigger than the other, and his wrinkled face is now flushed red.

Lexi walks right up to him. "Hello, Mr. Jasper," she says.

Mr. Jasper looks at her for a second. Then, with a scratchy sigh, he points at a chair next to him.

"Sit down!" he orders.

Lexi nods and plops into the chair. Jake joins them, sitting in a nearby chair.

"Did you grow up in Carrolton, sir?" asks Jake respectfully.

"I was born here, yes," says Mr. Jasper. "And with any luck, *I'll die here too*. Ha!"

"Horace is pretty *feisty* for eighty-seven, wouldn't you say?" says Bob, wiping a glass case full of scissors and clipper attachments.

"*Eighty-seven?*" Lexi gasps.

Mr. Jasper gives her a squinty look. "Does my age *disturb* you, missy?"

"Yes," says Lexi.

"So what can you tell us about Blackwater Estate?" asks Jake eagerly.

"It's haunted!" Mr. Jasper says. His big eye grows small, and his small eye grows big.

Nobody speaks for a few seconds. Then Jake clears his throat. Still nobody speaks.

"Haunted," repeats Jake finally.

"Yes!" Mr. Jasper shouts.

"Wow," says Jake, nodding. "Any details on that?"

"Maybe, but first, tell me why you're so *interested*," says Mr. Jasper.

"We . . . saw the mansion," Jake replies carefully.

"How?" says Mr. Jasper.

"From the spillway," says Jake. "You know, where the creek exits the Enclave neighborhood?"

Mr. Jasper nods. "Clever," he states. "Very clever indeed. Clever as a fox!"

Jake and Lexi exchange a look. Lexi shrugs.

"Well, we were following someone," she explains.

Jake cringes a bit. He thinks, *The girl is an open book.*

"*Who?*" asks Mr. Jasper with urgency. "Who were you following?"

"Some old guy," replies Jake.

"Why?"

Jake starts to speak again, but Lexi cuts in too quickly. She says, "We were worried about him. He didn't have a coat or hat, and it was really cold."

Jake hesitates, then smiles. "Okay," he says. "Sure. Let's go with that."

Mr. Jasper thinks about this a minute. "So this old fellow led you to the Enclave spillway?" he says.

"Actually, he got over the wall and into the estate itself," says Jake. "I'm not sure how, but I saw him heading up to the mansion."

Now Bob the Barber's interest goes up a notch. He stops wiping counters. "You saw an old man going to Blackwater House?" His voice rumbles with intensity. "Are you sure?"

"Yes," says Jake. "Is that odd?"

"Yes, that's odd!" Mr. Jasper yells.

"Jake, that house has been deserted for at least three years," says Bob. "Some brouhaha about the family will. Legal problems, I believe."

"Well, it's not deserted now," Jake tells him. "I saw limousines in the driveway, and the place was lit up like a night at the opera."

Bob considers this. "Well," he says. "That's very interesting."

"And we know his name, too!" says Lexi, bobbing her head up and down. Jake has never seen Lexi so talkative.

"The old man's name?" Bob asks.

"Yes," says Lexi. "Mr. Latimer said it was a guy named Old Dan something."

Mr. Jasper drops his fishing magazine.

Bob drops into the empty barber chair, stunned and clearly upset. "Dunnagin?"

"That's it."

"That's impossible," says Bob. "You must have heard wrong."

Jake shrugs. "Well, Mr. Latimer told us the guy's blind, so I guess it doesn't make much sense."

Mr. Jasper squawks out a mirthless laugh. "Blind?" he screams. "*I'll* say he's blind!"

Bob shakes his big head and says, "Jake . . . Old Dan passed away last July."

6

WOLVES AND A DOG

Go Team One

Cyril listens nervously to the chatter between Lucas and Cat on his Spy Link channel. Cat is inside the ice arena; Lucas is next to Cyril outside the entrance. Cyril looks a little haggard and sneezes yet again. This time, however, he covers his Spy Link mouthpiece.

What about up there? asks Cat.

"Roger that, Charlie Kilo," Lucas says. "Unclear on your placement coordinates. Can you give us some transmit data for target lock verification?"

There is a pause. Then Cat says, **Who are you talking to?**

"You," Lucas says.

Another pause. Then: **Oh.**

Cyril suddenly slaps Lucas's arm. "Bogies at three o'clock!" he says, pointing.

The two boys dive behind a landscape retaining wall near the arena entrance. Both quickly dig Micro Periscopes out of their coat pockets and use them to spy unseen over the top of the wall. Several Wolf Pack members jog up to Swank Ice Arena's main doors, led by Brill Joseph.

"My God, they're ugly," Cyril whispers, watching.

"Girl recon unit, be advised," whispers Lucas into his Spy Link mouthpiece. "We have Whiskey Papa on a hot approach vector. Repeat, Whiskey Papa approaching."

Will you knock it off, Bixby? says Cat's voice over the channel.

"Cat, the Wolf Pack's entering the arena," translates Cyril. "Plant the dang gadget and get out of sight."

"Don't forget to turn it on," Lucas says.

Already done, she says.

"Cool," says Lucas.

He stows his periscope, slings his gadget backpack down behind the wall, and opens it. Then he pulls out a remote control unit with an antenna and two joysticks. Attached by wire to the unit is a headset that looks like bizarre eyeglasses. A small, square eyepiece—actually a mini video screen—sits over the right eye.

Lucas slides this headset onto his face. "Point the car at something," he says.

Okay, replies Cat.

On the eyepiece Lucas watches a live black-and-white video feed of Swank Arena's main ice rink. Then the view pans in a circle and ends up on Cat's face.

So this is an actual video camera, here on the front of the car? she asks, holding it closer to her eye for inspection.

"Yes," says Lucas, watching her eye blink.

Can you see me?

"Your cornea is frightening."

Sweet!

Now Lucas watches the camera view swing upward. He sees a big horizontal support beam near the ceiling. It runs the full length of the arena, wall to wall. Several V-shaped struts extend from the beam upward and attach to the ceiling.

See that big beam over the ice? asks Cat.

"I do."

See how it goes clear down to the end of the building?

Cat pans the camera down the support beam. It runs directly over the rink.

"I see," Lucas says.

If you can drive the car along the beam, says Cat, then tilt the camera downward a bit, you should be able to survey the ice.

"Excellent!" says Lucas. "Yes, yes, the camera angle is manually adjustable. Go ahead—tilt it as far down as possible."

The live video feed swivels back toward Cat. The picture bounces wildly as she reaches toward the camera and makes the adjustment.

Okay, all set, she says.

"Intense," says Cyril. "Can you reach the beam?"

Yes. I'm standing on a big exit sign just underneath it.

Cyril raises a fist. "What an impressive chunk of womanly badness you are," he shouts.

I am magnificent, admits Cat.

"Better hurry," says Lucas.

Don't worry, they can't see me up here, Cat says. Okay, I got the car up.

In his eyepiece display, Lucas sees the top of the support beam stretching ahead, flat and wide and clear as an interstate highway. The camera's downward angle cuts off some of the long view, but Lucas can see far enough ahead to drive the vehicle.

Smiling with joy, he pushes a joystick forward on the remote control unit.

Dude, your car's moving, says Cat. I'm hopping down now. Ah yes, Brill and the cretins are just getting on the ice.

Lucas steers the Spy Video Car along the support beam a few feet. Then, as a test, he carefully turns it ninety degrees left, facing perpendicular to the beam. He jogs the vehicle forward slowly, bit by bit, until the camera sees over the edge of the beam.

Lucas gasps.

On his eyepiece, in full video splendor, he watches the Wolf Pack go through their broomball warm-ups on the ice below.

Go Team Two

Back in the barbershop, Jake tries to grasp what he's hearing. But it's not easy being told you saw a dead guy.

"You're telling me . . . we saw a dead guy?" he asks Bob.

"No," says Bob. "I'm just telling you it couldn't have been Old Dan." He shakes his head. "Mr. Latimer must have been mistaken."

"Lights in Blackwater House," Mr. Jasper croaks with momentous drama.

"Alarming," says Bob grimly.

Old Mr. Jasper nods. "And so the lost heir has returned!"

Jake turns to him. "The what?"

Bob gets up from his chair. "The heir," he says. "The inheritor of the Blackwater Estate."

"He's back," moans Mr. Jasper, eyes wide. "*Just as it was foretold.*"

Jake attempts to take this seriously. "Who foretold it?"

"I don't know!" Mr. Jasper howls, looking devastated.

Jake nods. "Okay."

"It's a local legend," explains Bob. "The story is that the son of Harliss Blackwater left town after a violent falling-out with his father. This would have been way back in the 1950s."

"Violent?" Lexi says, looking anxious.

"Yes," says Bob. He picks up a straight razor and starts sharpening it on a leather strop. "Some say the old man killed his son, because the younger Blackwater disappeared after the fight. But other folks claim to have seen him over the years, lurking about town, acting strange."

"They say he *comes and goes*," gorkles[7] Mr. Jasper.

Bob nods. "Biding his time," he says mysteriously. "Waiting." Still holding the razor, he sits back down in the empty chair.

"For what?" asks Jake.

Bob shrugs. "Nobody knows," he says mysteriously. "Revenge, maybe."

"Revenge against his father?" asks Jake.

"No," says Bob mysteriously. "No, Harliss Blackwater is long dead."

Jake squints and scratches his head. "Then, uh . . . who does he want revenge against?"

Bob looks off mysteriously into the distance.

"Nobody knows," he says.

---

7. I'm running out of words to describe how Mr. Jasper speaks, so now I'm making them up.

"It's a mystery!" skreeks Mr. Jasper.

Suddenly a muffled voice rises from the hot towel wrapped on the customer's face.

"Does this come off," asks the voice, "or do I just wear it home?"

Lexi recognizes the voice. Her eyes grow big.

"Oh, right," Bob says, leaping to his feet. "Time to shave." He leans over the customer and whips off the hot towel.

Jake and Lexi stare in disbelief at the face underneath.

"Do your homework, Bixby," says the flush-faced customer. "I'll give you five bucks if you actually get smart."

"Marco, you cut your hair," Jake replies. "Wow. I'm trying not to laugh."

Lexi looks appalled.

"It's all gone," she says.

Using a Silvertip badger-bristle brush, Bob starts dabbing shaving soap on Marco's chin in small, gentle circular motions. "You know these kids?" he asks Marco.

The answer of course is yes. Marco, as every fool knows, was Team Spy Gear's first nemesis way back in Book 1 of this remarkable, powerfully written series. Since then he has turned into a formidable and loyal ally. Marco's computer hacking skills are renowned in the cyberworld. His trademark tangle of dreadlocks combined with his ragged, hulking presence once made him look monstrous and menacing. Indeed, in

Book 1 the team mistook him for the legendary Farmer's Monster. And in Book 3, the Wolf Pack mistook him for the legendary Wild Axman of Killicut County. There's stuff in other books, too, but I forgot it, although I'm sure it's brilliantly written. Anyway, now Marco's hair is short and neatly trimmed, and he looks almost human.

"You look human, almost," says Jake, who I'm pretty sure just heard me say that, but changed the word order to avoid a plagiarism lawsuit.

"You look like George Clooney!" blurts Lexi.

Marco nods. "Wow. A compliment from the spunky little girl."

"I hate George Clooney," Lexi says.

Bob swirls his brush to work the soap into a rich lather, completely covering the lower half of Marco's face. Something starts beeping across the room—four short beeps, then a long beep.

"Uh-oh," says Jake. He looks at Lexi. "What code is that?"

"Red alert," Lexi answers.

"Crud!" Jake rushes to his coat, which he'd hung on a coat peg as he came in the door. He rips open a Velcro pocket and extracts a walkie-talkie unit. Then he presses a button and says, "Talk to me, over."

Roger, uh, well . . . it's . . . me. Over. It's Lucas, and he sounds very subdued.

"Roger that, Lima Bravo," says Jake. He knows his brother well. "What's wrong, dude? Over."

Here we need to take a short step backward in time to bring you up to date on Go Team One.

Go Team One

Ten minutes ago: Lucas is steering the sleek Spy Video Car down the arena's support beam. He wants to get it closer to the beam's midpoint for a wider view of the Wolf Pack's workout below.

"Can you see the vehicle?" Lucas asks. "Can you hear it? It's not too obvious up there, is it?"

I hear nothing but the Neanderthal grunting of beefy thugs, says Cat over the Spy Link. Don't worry—there's no way they can see your car from the ice.

Lucas relaxes a bit. This Spy Video Car is pretty much the most amazing, insanely sick gadget that he's ever seen, and he loves it . . . *loves it*, I tell you. Ever since finding the vehicle and its components tucked inside a closed locker behind the gadget shelf at Stoneship HQ, he's longed to field-test the device.

Tapping the remote control joysticks with expert precision, Lucas carefully turns the car and inches it closer to the edge of the beam. When the downward-tilted camera lens clears the edge, Lucas immediately stops the car. The view reveals only about one-third of the rink below.

"Good enough," says Lucas.

"Can you see the rink?" Cyril asks him.

"Some of it," Lucas replies.

"Then here," says Cyril. He hands Lucas the Spy Gear Casebook. "Take notes."

Watching the helmet-clad Wolves scrimmage, Lucas whips out a pen. Then he jots down several quick observations. Here's a summation:

One, the Pack is vicious. Hooking. Tripping. Grabbing. Sticks go high, often. Wilson Wills is a master of slashing.

Two, they tend to attack one-on-one, with very little passing or teamwork.

Three, Brill's defensive skills are brutal and effective . . . but he tends to chase the ball, ignoring attackers who pass and then glide off into space for a return "give-and-go" pass. *This can be exploited,* thinks Lucas.

Finally, Lucas notices that Brill often leaves his stance wide open when checking an attacker. This makes Lucas smile really big.

Yes, all this is obvious to Lucas's keen eye after just five minutes. But the edge of the support beam cuts off much of the rink from his view. Lucas gently taps the joystick forward. The Spy Video Car creeps an inch closer to the edge.

"Just a *little* more ice," says Lucas. "We need to see their overall team shape and strategy."

Just as Lucas taps the stick again, something beeps in his backpack.

Guess what?

It's the Omega Link again.

Unfortunately, few things excite Lucas more than an Omega Link beep. It means another message, another clue from some shadowy agent of intrigue. It always gives him a jolt of energy.

And thus he taps the joystick a *little* too hard.

"Aaaaaagggh!" he cries, watching the rink rise up fast.

"What?" Cyril says in alarm.

Crap, your car just fell! cries Cat. **Right on the flipping ice!**

Seen through the eyepiece, the car's fall makes Lucas's stomach drop. After a couple of bounces, the vehicle settles upside down on the rink's edge, facing the nearby boards. Amazingly, the camera isn't broken; it continues its live feed with good clarity. But wheels up, the Video Spy Car is not maneuverable. For a few desperate seconds, Lucas actually hopes it won't be discovered. But then he hears Cat in his ear.

Yo, Bixby, they're heading for the car now, she says.

"Gosh darn it!" yells Lucas.

Suddenly the video view flips right side up and swivels. And there, leering into the camera, is the toothy, pockmarked horror-fest that is Brill Joseph's face.

Lucas screams and fights the urge to rip the headset off.

Brill's got your car, says Cat.

"I . . . see that," says Lucas, recovering.

Let's just hope he's too stupid to figure out what it is, Cat adds.

Now Lucas fights nausea as the live camera feed starts swaying this way and that. In jerky video, he watches various Wolf Pack members examine the car, shake it, sniff it, lick it, then howl hideously and pass it on.

Meanwhile, Cyril digs the beeping Omega Link out of the gadget backpack. He holds it up and reads the single word on the view screen:

ECOPHAGY

"Ecophagy?" he says. He looks over at Lucas. "It says ecophagy." He bobs his head. "What a word. Yeah. One of my favorites."

Lucas watches as the video feed jounces across the ice to one of the rinkside player benches. He catches a jerky glimpse of coats and bags. Then, suddenly, the screen goes black.

Not good, says Cat.

"What happened?" Lucas asks, panicked.

Your baby's gone, says Cat. Brill just put it in his duffel bag.

"Cyril, I've lost the Video Spy Car," says Lucas, feeling

physically crushed. He tenses his fingers on the remote control.

"Well, isn't that just *ecophagy?*" says Cyril. "Ouch, it gets me right here"—he bangs on his chest—"right in the left ecophagy."

Cyril jabs the Omega Link at Lucas.

"Here," he says. *"You* figure it out."

Lucas looks at the Omega display. Then he pulls out his walkie-talkie and makes the forlorn call to Jake.

And that brings us back to the present.

Go Team Three

This was a test. Ha!

There is no Go Team Three, of course.

If you forgot that fact, please put down the book and beat yourself with a stick. Be sure to use good technique, or I'll start writing in Vedic Sanskrit, which takes seven years to translate.

Go Team Two

Jake, I lost the Spy Video Car, Lucas reports over the walkie-talkie. The sound of his voice crackles sadly across the barbershop.

"What do you mean, you *lost* it?" asks Jake. "Over."

I drove it and, uh, it fell, Lucas replies. Like, onto the rink. Then Brill found it. Over.

"Roger," says Jake. "That's . . . bad news."

There is a pause. "Over," Lexi reminds him.

"Oh, right," says Jake. "Over."[8]

Also, we got another weird Omega message, adds Lucas. In the barber chair, Marco suddenly sits up straight, listening. Another dang word to look up. Pause. Crackling sounds. Then: Cyril's pretty disgusted with the dang thing right now. Over.

"What's the word? Over," asks Jake, glancing at Marco.

E-C-O-P-H-A-G-Y, Lucas spells. Ecophagy. Over.

Marco hops off the chair. "That message came through the Omega Link?" he asks with sudden concern. "Verify, please."

Jake nods okay at Marco. "Uh, Lima Bravo, can I get verification?" he says. "This word, 'ecophagy'—that's an Omega message, correct? Over."

"Affirmative, over," replies Lucas.

"Crap," Marco says. He jumps to his feet and yanks off the barber cape. Then he uses it to wipe the shaving cream off his face.

"Ecophagy is bad?" asks Jake, concerned by Marco's sense of urgency.

Marco says, "Tell him to meet us at Stoneship in twenty minutes." He reaches in his pocket, pulls out a twenty dollar bill, and jabs it at Bob. "Keep the change," he says.

8. Tip: In walkie-talkie communications, always say "Over" when you're finished with your turn to let the other party know that he/she can talk now. You can also say "Goats." Or the one I like to use in my personal walkie-talkie conversations: "Idiot." Read this conversation between Luke and Jake, replacing "over" with "idiot," and you'll see what I mean.

Bob says, "Considering your hair, twenty won't cover it."

Marco gives him a look. "How much do you want?"

"Six hundred dollars."

Marco nods. "Bill me." He glances over at Jake and Lexi, who watch him in wonder. "Let's *go*, children," he says.

"Is this a situation?" asks Jake.

"Oh, most certainly," Marco says with a grim look.

Lexi's eyes light up. "Situations" are some of her favorite things. "Will we need to climb something?" she asks.

As Marco hustles out the barbershop door, he plucks his coat from a wall peg and looks back. "If this message means what I think it does, the answer would be yes."

Happy, Lexi pulls on her purple stocking cap.

Go Team One

Lucas and Cyril trudge down the snowpacked bicycle path that runs along County Road 44. Lucas is still dejected about the Spy Video Car, but the prospect of a Stoneship meeting with Marco raises his spirits a bit.

Cyril walks bent forward, hands clasped behind his back.

"Ever think about certain words?" he asks. "Like 'lemon,' for example. What guy invented this word? Lemon, lemon, lemon, lemon, lemon, lemon, lemon, lemon, lemon, lemon. After a while, it stops making sense. It's just a weird sound." Cyril shakes his head. "This disturbs me."

"Why?" asks Lucas.

"Because lemons are so sour."

Lucas turns to stare at Cyril. Cyril starts whistling and gazing up at trees along the bike path.

"Cyril," says Lucas.

"Yeah?"

"I don't get it."

"Get what?"

"Your point about lemons."

Cyril looks perplexed. "I have no idea what you're talking about," he says.

Lucas tries not to grit his teeth. Key character trait: *Lucas Bixby doesn't like things left hanging, unfinished, unresolved.* (Note to SparkNotes people: Feel free to use this insight.)

"Look," says Lucas doggedly, "what does a lemon's sourness have to do with—"

Suddenly a loud, guttural growl rumbles from a clump of juniper maybe thirty yards up ahead, next to the bike path. It sounds canine, and sure enough, a second later a large black dog emerges, its teeth bared. But there's an odd quality to the sound.

Lucas stares at the dog. "Listen," he says quietly to Cyril. "Hear that?"

Cyril is frozen in place. "Hear what?" he murmurs.

The dog growls again. Then it starts to spin around, as if chasing its tail. It stops, and its head twists sideways at an unnatural angle. Baring its teeth again, the dog shudders, then starts twisting its head side to side, whining.

Then it growls deeply again, and Cyril hears it.

"An echo?" he says.

Both boys stare at the dog.

"That growl isn't coming from his throat," says Lucas.

Indeed, although the sound comes from the direction of the dog, it seems to emanate more from the space the dog occupies—as if transmitted by big speakers—rather than from its throat.

"It sounds like, like . . . a stereo recording," says Lucas.

"That's it, exactly," Cyril agrees.

Suddenly the black dog barks. The bark is so deep and powerful that the ground shakes.

Lucas and Cyril are paralyzed with fright.

"That . . . is not a natural bark," says Lucas.

"No," says Cyril. "It's not."

Despite his fear, Lucas finds himself fascinated by the phenomenon. "It sounds like a high-decibel, low-frequency playback of a recorded bark," he says.

"It gives new meaning to the concept of woofers," says Cyril.

"How can we scare him off?" asks Lucas.

Cyril swallows a lump. "Maybe we can use my hair in some unusual manner," he says hoarsely.

The dog's head rolls side to side again, looking rubbery,

almost elastic. Its eyes are milky white and seem about to pop from the black head. The animal spins again, remarkably fast, around and around, whining loudly.

"You think it has rabies?" asks Lucas.

"It sounds . . . in pain, doesn't it?" says Cyril, feeling a twinge of pity.

All of a sudden the black dog shoots off at an astounding rate of speed. It bounds like a champion greyhound over the snow beside the bike path, heading south toward Stoneship Woods. Without a second thought, Cyril and Lucas set off in pursuit.

"Holy cow, he's a jet!" cries Lucas.

"We're losing him," Cyril pants. "Dang, he's so fast it looks like he's not even touching the ground."

This comment strikes Lucas. "Hey, you're absolutely right," he says. He stops and points where the dog ran. "I don't see any paw prints, do you?"

Cyril nods and gazes up ahead. "Look, he's spinning again!"

Up ahead, in the parking lot of a small office building, the black dog circles and starts howling with the decibel power of a civil defense siren. The sound is piercing.

"What the blazes is wrong with him?" asks Lucas, covering his ears.

The boys remain a safe distance from the dog.

"Now look at him," says Cyril. "He's . . . glimmering."

"It's his coat!" Lucas exclaims. "It's rippling."

Some kind of odd silvery glow passes over the dog. Then the animal freezes—almost literally, it seems. It stands like an ice statue. But after a few seconds, it recovers and darts off around the office building.

"Wow!" shouts Cyril.

"Come on!" calls Lucas.

The two boys round the building hot on the black dog's trail. On the other side is a big, snowy field, about three acres of open space. The dog is nowhere to be seen.

"What?" says Cyril. "Where'd he go?"

Lucas sees a circle of disturbed snow. Remembering the circles along the trail of the old man yesterday, he approaches it. Suddenly, flakes burst upward from the circle like a hissing explosion, and then just as quickly drop.

Both boys stop moving.

"Okay," says Lucas, spooked. He points at the circle. "Now *that's* not right."

"Yes, I'm pretty convinced we should go home now," Cyril says. He starts backing away. "I've never seen such *angry* snow before."

But Lucas Bixby can't help it. He steps closer.

Nothing happens.

He steps again. Nothing. Then he steps to the edge of the circle.

As he does, a white mist rises slowly from the spot.

The mist drifts toward Lucas, then starts swirling around him. Now he feels a stinging sensation—in his eyes, his nose, his throat, all over his body, in fact. He starts coughing.

"You're in some kind of swarm!" shouts Cyril. "Get out! Run this way!"

But before Lucas can move, the mist floats away from him. It gathers nearby into a white shape like a fluid apparition or a ghost. Both boys distinctly hear the entity hiss. Then suddenly it speeds off across the open field.

In a second, it is gone.

7

GRAY GOO

Marco and the kids sit on the floor of the Stoneship HQ control room. Both Go Teams have made their full reports. Now everyone stares off into space with troubled faces. Cyril, in particular, looks bad. His eyes are wet, droopy, and bloodshot. Jake notices.

"Dude, your eyes are hideous," he tells Cyril.

"Thanks," says Cyril. "And hey, you should see my femur! It's ghastly." He sneezes violently.

Jake grins but still looks concerned. "I think you've caught that flu going around," he says. "Yeah, we need to get you home."

"No, Jake," says Cyril. "I need to run through the forest in the dead of winter some more. That would really bolster my immune system."

Nearby, Lucas clears his throat, again and again. The stinging is gone, but he feels a lingering itch. "Virtual dogs," he says, shaking his head. "Dissolving birds. Are we all going insane?"

"Let's not forget the hostile, hissing snowflakes," mumbles Cyril miserably. "Now *that's* depressing. Imagine trying to ski on that stuff."

Jake turns to Cyril. "And Marco hasn't even told you guys about *ecophagy* yet."

Cyril looks over at Marco and says, "Is it bad?"

Marco nods.

"Then don't tell me," says Cyril.

Marco cracks a thin smile. "When you find yourself decomposing into gray goo, you might want to know why it's happening." He glances at Cyril's head. "The only thing left would be your hair. Nothing could decompose that."

Cyril sneezes again. "And how did Bob cut *yours* off?" he asks, wiping his nose. "With a chainsaw?"

"Tell them about the goo," says Lexi. She sounds a bit worried.

"Sure." Marco stands up. "So I heard about your first Omega Link message," he says to Lucas and Cyril.

"Nanite?" says Lucas.

"Right," Marco replies. "Nanite." He folds his arms, thinking.

"Marco," says Lexi. "The goo."

"I'm getting to it." He looks at Jake. "Didn't you wonder who sent you this message?"

"Not really," says Jake. "We figured it was the Agency. Or maybe another Agency mole in Viper's organization, like last time." A little embarrassed, he turns to the other kids. "Huh. I guess we never really discussed it."

Kids, you can skip the following two paragraphs. They provide a quick recap for your parents, who probably didn't read Book 3: *The Quantum Quandary* or, if they did, they're too busy to remember, plus they're old, and some of them are starting to smell bad.

First: Viper, of course, is the shadowy, ruthless nemesis who originally hired Marco to bring down the Internet back in Book 1: *The Secret of Stoneship Woods*. Since then, Viper has tried to wreak global havoc using advanced technologies, only to be thwarted at every turn by Team Spy Gear. This being a Spy Gear Adventure, it seems exceedingly odd that we've finished more than six chapters, and yet here's the first mention of Viper in this book. Very odd indeed. Very suspicious.

Second: The Agency mentioned by Jake Bixby is an equally shadowy government intelligence group, the same one we mentioned back in Chapter 3. This black ops unit has been hunting Viper for years. Beyond that, little else is known of its murky agenda. In the last Spy Gear adventure, an Agency mole managed to infiltrate one of Viper's top secret laboratories and then send out coded warnings via the Omega Link.

Whew!

Parents, please go back to your jobs now.

Marco is lost in thought again. After a few more seconds, he says, "Say the contact *is* from the Agency. Why are these bozos sending such troubling messages to *you*?"

Jake shrugs. "Because we're good?" he suggests.

Marco says, "You're not *that* good."

"Says who?" chirps Lexi.

Marco looks at her.

"Anyway, the first message was nanite," Lucas says. "Why is that so troubling?"

"Did you research it?" asks Marco.

"Yes," Lucas replies. "Nanites are little microrobots, not much bigger than molecules. What does that have to do with ecophagy?"

Marco goes to the console and sits in the leather captain's chair at the main monitor. "Ecophagy is a fairly recent term," he says. "It means, literally, eating the planet."

"Eating dirt?" asks Lucas.

"No," says Marco. "Eating the *entire* planet."

"What could eat an entire planet?" Cyril wonders. "I mean, other than a Karkadian Warrbokk."

"A self-replicating nanite swarm, gone out of control," says Marco.

Lucas frowns. "Explain," he says.

Marco poises his fingers over the console keyboard. "Intelligent, aggressive nanoswarms that consume entire planets or even galaxies have been the stuff of science fiction for years," he says.

"Like the Borg in *Star Trek*," says Lucas.

"Right," says Marco. "Well, the theory's not so totally sci-fi anymore. Current nanotech research is letting us imagine scary things. Like smart swarms of nanorobots that use distributed group intelligence to learn and evolve."

Lucas frowns. "What's distributed group intelligence?" he asks.

"It's complicated," explains Marco. "In a nutshell, it means that one nanorobot isn't so smart, but a hundred billion nanorobots working together in a neural swarm can become very, *very* smart." He types quickly. "It's like Einstein's brain."

"What do you mean?" Lucas asks, fascinated.

"Well, if you took just one of Einstein's brain cells, it wouldn't be too brilliant, not by itself," says Marco. "But put *all* of 'em together into a neural network and you can get a genius." He nods. "Eventually, anyway. Once the Einstein brain learns how to think."

"So a swarm of nanites can be as smart as Einstein?" asks Lucas.

"Oh, much smarter," says Marco. "Theoretically, anyway.

For one, there's no limit to how big a nanoswarm can grow. Imagine a brain the size of the Milky Way. Plus you could program certain high-level math functions into even a small swarm, giving it the computational abilities of a supercomputer."

"That's kind of a creepy thought," says Lucas.

Cyril sneezes. Then he says, "Please don't tell my mom about this math-fog monster." He wipes his nose. "She'll want to buy one for me."

Lucas clears his throat again. "Good gosh," he says to Marco. "Are you saying that's what Cyril and I saw? That white fog was a swarm of nanites?"

"Possibly," says Marco.

"But the stuff we read says nanorobot technology is still years, maybe decades away," Lucas says.

"It is," Marco admits.

Lucas points through the big window down at the warehouse door. "Then how could that be a *nanoswarm* out there?"

"It couldn't," says Marco. "That's what's troubling. Because the thing you describe sure *sounds* like a nanoswarm." Marco swivels the chair toward the kids. "You know, a smart swarm is one thing. But a swarm able to physically mimic what it encounters in nature?" He runs a hand through his short hair. "That's inconceivable."

"Is it alive?" Lexi asks.

Cyril points at her. "Excellent question for such a small child," he says.

"Could someone be controlling it?" Lucas puts in. "Or is it a self-directed swarm?"

Marco ignores these questions and starts typing rapidly; the keys clatter with machine-gun precision. For a few seconds he is lost in his work.

"Marco," says Lexi.

"*What?*"

"Tell them about the gray goo," Lexi insists.

Marco gives her an irritated look. But he turns to Cyril and Lucas and says, "Okay, listen. Keep in mind that this is *entirely* hypothetical."

"We promise not to laugh," says Cyril.

"Gray goo is a term coined in the early days of nano-technology research," Marco begins. "This guy named Eric Drexler described an ecophagy scenario. It starts with a swarm of nanomachines programmed to self-replicate—to scavenge matter from the ecosystem, tear it apart at the cellular level, and then use the pieces to build copies of itself.

"In Drexler's scenario, something goes wrong. The trigger could be an error—an accidental mutation, say—or maybe sabotage, or even a deliberate doomsday war device. In any case, the swarm kicks into a nonstop replica-tion frenzy. It attacks and breaks down every living organ-ism on Earth into a gray chemical soup that the swarm's internal nanofactories can feed on to build copies of itself."

"Hence, gray goo," says Lucas.

Cyril sneezes. "Okay, kill me now," he wheezes.

Jake is thoughtful. After a few seconds, he says, "Marco, you say this is just hypothetical, like a science fiction concept."

"Yes."

"Then why these Omega Link messages about nanites and ecophagy?" asks Jake. "I mean, doesn't that sound like a *warning* to you?"

"Yes, it does," says Marco. "Exactly what I'm trying to get at."

Now Lucas asks what everybody is wondering: "Do you think . . . Viper is behind any of this?" He gives a worried glance at his brother.

"Seems like his kind of fun," says Jake, nodding.

Marco gazes at the monitor, checks a result that pops up onscreen, then shakes his head. "I find no trace of Agency chatter in my usual contact locations," he says, gesturing at the screen. "I mean, if Viper's involved and this is such a dire situation, *where are they?*"

Jake shrugs. "Maybe they're just lying low," he guesses.

"Or maybe they're out of commission, for some reason," says Marco. "In any case, I think we're facing a technology that's *way* out of our league, that nobody thought was possible for another ten or twenty years."

Cyril sneezes loudly. He pulls Kleenex from his

pocket and honks his nose. Then he lies flat on his back, next to the floor hatch. "Say, does anybody else feel that nearby lava flow?"

Marco reaches down and lays his huge, hairy hand on Cyril's forehead.

"Yep," he says. "This kid's burning up."

Jake hops to his feet. "Okay, let's scoot." He looks at Lucas. "Well, things sort of make sense now, don't they? All that weird stuff we've been seeing. It's all related."

"Everything spins," says Lexi.

Jake stares at her. "Holy goats!" he cries.

Lucas says, "What?"

Now Jake stares at Lucas. "The snow devils spin," he says. "The birds spin. The black dog spins."

Lexi jumps up. "Old Dan spins!" she exclaims.

"*Precisely*," says Jake.

"My gosh," Lucas says in a hushed tone. "That's right. The old guy kept spinning around, making those circles in the snow."

Lexi looks stunned. "Old Dan is a swarm?"

Cyril, still on his back staring at the ceiling, raises a finger. "That would explain how a blind dead guy could hop walls," he says. He sits up and repeatedly blows his nose. It sounds like geese arguing.

Behind Cyril, a wisp of black smoke slowly floats up through the open floor hatch.

Jake is thoughtful as he pulls on his coat. "Do you

suppose Blackwater House has anything to do with this nanobusiness?" he asks. "I mean, Old Dan . . . or his nanoghost, or whatever it was . . . well, we saw it heading for the mansion."

Lucas frowns. "Maybe it was just hopping the wall and cutting across the estate property to lose us. It certainly worked."

"Right," says Jake. "But those white limos and gray guys were pretty creepy."

"It looked entirely normal to me," Cyril says. "Look, everybody knows that superrich people all belong to weird cults and secret societies and stuff."

Lexi looks earnestly at Marco.

"Marco?" she asks.

Marco rolls his eyes. "How many times are you going to *bellow* my name today?"

Lexi pulls nervously on her fingers. "Can we hide from it?" she asks.

"The swarm?"

"Yes, the swarm."

Marco sees her unease. "Well, uh . . . no," he answers. "Because of their submicron size, nanite particles can infiltrate almost anything. A room would have to be perfectly sealed. . . ."

Cyril suddenly notices more black smoke drifting up through the hatch. "Crap!" he says in alarm. "Is something burning?"

As the others turn to look, the smoke gets thicker and starts swirling slowly around Cyril.

"Ahhhh!" cries Cyril, waving frantically at the smoke. "Dang! It's stinging my eyes!"

Suddenly the smoke flashes silver, twice.

Jake leaps forward. "That's no smoke!" he shouts.

"It's the swarm!" cries Lucas, scrambling after Jake.

Instinctively, both Bixby boys wade into the swirling black fog, wildly flapping their hands, trying to dissipate it. Lexi and Marco dive in too; Marco whips off his jacket and tries to fan the smoke away. But unlike real smoke, this fog seems to absorb each flailing movement, flowing around hands and arms like an oily gas. Soon everyone is coughing.

"It's in my throat!" coughs Lexi.

"My eyes!" Lucas cries, rubbing frantically at them.

"Keep swinging!" calls Jake fiercely. "Don't stop!"

In the midst of this madness, Cyril is gripped by an uncontrollable sneezing fit.

"Aaaahhhh-*chooo! Achoo!*"

The black fog recoils from Cyril.

"Ahhh-choo! *Achoo, achoo, achoo!* Holy crap! I can't stop! Ahhhhhhhh-*choooo!*"

The others watch the fog.

"What's it doing?" gasps Jake. "Marco?"

"I don't . . . know," Marco coughs.

Cyril falls to his knees, holding his nose. The black

fog pulsates a few times, like a beating heart, then suddenly changes colors to a brilliant white. Two misty tendrils curl out of the main body of bright smoke, reaching tentatively toward Cyril. As they get close, Cyril releases his nose and starts swatting at them.

"Haaaaaa-*chawww!*" he sneezes, right into the swarm.

The smoky tendrils retract back into the main body of the mist.

Abruptly, the entity shoots downward through the hatch, as if suctioned by a powerful vacuum.

Jake staggers to the window overlooking the warehouse floor. He sees the churning smoke speed toward the south cargo door. But as it moves, it starts splintering into smaller, jagged wisps.

"It's breaking up!" shouts Jake.

The others rush to the window, except for Cyril, who is wracked by another sneezing fit.

"Look!" Lucas exclaims, pointing at the open cargo door.

The shattered wisps snake out past a large, dark figure silhouetted in the doorway.

8

THE MEETING

"Children," says Marco. "Meet the Dark Man."

A huge, black-caped figure climbs up through the floor hatch. Scary French horn music fills the room, with lots of really scary low notes and such.[9] The man's face is hidden by dark sunglasses plus a black polysulphone mask over his nose and mouth. A small air-feed hose runs from the mask to an oxygen pack attached at his waist. The man also wears a wide-brimmed black hat pulled low.

"Aren't you taking your Darth Vader obsession a little far?" Cyril asks.

"I see you've *matured* . . . since our last meeting, Mr. Wong," rasps the man as he struggles to his feet with some difficulty. "This is a breathing apparatus, for your information."

9. Am I the only person who finds French horns frightening?

The Dark Man slowly approaches Cyril. He's at least six and a half feet tall, and broad as a linebacker.

"Don't hit me," says Cyril.

The Dark Man's digital voice filter warps the sound of his labored breathing into a harsh, robotic hiss. "The Agency has been afflicted . . . with a pulmonary disorder of . . . suspicious origin," he gasps.

"You have breathing problems?" asks Jake, stepping forward.

"That's correct, Mr. Bixby," says the Dark Man.

Cyril appraises his cloak. "Do you guys wear black *pajamas*, too?"

The Dark Man leans down to Cyril. "Hmmm, you sound horrible," he observes.

Cyril leans away. "Yes, but at least I sound human."

"I wear an LP voice-filter mask," says the Dark Man. "What's *your* excuse?"

"I'm sick," Cyril answers. "I feel like dog food gone bad." He thinks for a second. "Or maybe it's good food, but for bad dogs. It's bad, whatever it is, and there's dogs involved. I'm not sure why."

Lexi snorts out an involuntary laugh. Embarrassed, she clamps a hand over her mouth.

The Dark Man just looks at her for a second.

Jake eyes the intruder warily. "Well, the flu's been going around," he says.

"So I hear," says the Dark Man.

Marco stands by the window, looking down at the cargo door. "Did you see it leave?" he asks.

"Yes," rumbles the Dark Man. "It was breaking apart. What happened?"

"It attacked us!" blurts Lexi, her face flushed.

The Dark Man turns to her. "Attacked?" There is a note of concern in his voice.

Lexi nods vigorously.

"Were you afraid?" he asks.

"Totally," she says.

"How is your breathing?" asks the man.

"Kind of stinging," says Lexi. "But not too bad."

Marco reaches down and pats Lexi on the back. "It was pretty intense up here for a few seconds," he says to the Dark Man. Then he nods over at Cyril. "Until flu boy gave it a good spraying."

The Dark Man turns sharply to Marco. "What do you mean?"

As if on cue, Cyril sneezes. "Haaaaaa-*chaw!*"

Marco reaches into his coat pocket and pulls out a small pack of fresh Kleenex. "The swarm was all over him. But he had a sneezing fit, and it backed away." He tosses the Kleenex to Cyril. "Here you go, dude."

"Thanks," sniffles Cyril.

"Hmmmm," the Dark Man murmurs. "The flu. Interesting."

He fluffs out his black cape and leans back against the

console desk. Jake notices that his great dark shoulders sag a bit, as if weary. "The swarm withdrew when Mr. Wong started sneezing," he repeats.

"Correct," says Marco.

"Very odd," says the Dark Man.

"Yes," Marco agrees.

Jake can't stand it any longer. He takes a determined step forward.

"Sir?" he asks. "We really need to get Cyril home, but I have to ask you something."

The Dark Man considers this. "Yes, no doubt you have questions."

"Who are you?" asks Jake bluntly.

"I can't say," replies the Dark Man.

"Why are you here?"

"That's classified," the Dark Man says.

Cyril raises a finger. "Good start," he says. "I think we're really on the right track here."

"Okay, how about this?" says Jake. "What is the Agency? Like, why does it exist?"

The Dark Man folds his arms. After a few seconds, he answers, "Protection."

"Protection," repeats Jake.

"Yes."

"What are you protecting?"

"Everything," replies the Dark Man.

Jake looks frustrated. "How so?"

"I can't say."

Cyril snorts. "As your lawyer, I'd have to advise you to be more vague," he says. He gestures to Lucas and Lexi next to him. "You don't want to overwhelm these small children with actual information."

The Dark Man slides off the console desk and stands wordlessly, facing Cyril.

Cyril nods. "You're a *very large man*," he says.

"Why don't you ask me something I can answer?" suggests the Dark Man.

He looks over at Jake.

Jake thinks for a second, then tries again. "Do you work for the U.S. government?" he asks.

The Dark Man hesitates, then says, "That's a matter of interpretation."

Marco interrupts. "You know, that one really seemed like a yes-or-no type of question."

Looking down, the Dark Man rattles out a sigh through his filter mask. Then he looks up at Jake again. "For the sake of good faith, let's say yes. I work for the government. But *nothing* about this matter is quite that simple. There are interested parties everywhere." He glances at Marco. "And I do mean *everywhere*."

Jake takes a deep breath. "So . . . who is Viper?"

The Dark Man chuckles. Then he shakes his head and shrugs.

Jake is incredulous. "You don't *know*?"

"No."

"Where's he from?" asks Jake.

"Unknown."

"What's his agenda?" Cyril blurts.

The Dark Man shrugs. "Disruption," he says. "I would think this is apparent, even to you."

Cyril sits in the leather captain's chair. "Man, my head is pounding."

"But why is Viper disrupting stuff?" asks Lucas, hugging his gadget backpack protectively.

"To what exact purpose, Mr. Bixby, we can't say yet," replies the Dark Man. "But his recent access to hyper-advanced forms of technology is *extremely* unsettling and raises disturbing questions about both his resources and his contacts. Is he working for himself or as an agent of others? We don't know."

Lexi raises her hand. "I have one," she says.

The Dark Man looks at her. "Miss Lopez?"

She stands. "What's he look like?"

"Viper?" rumbles the Dark Man.

"Yeah," Lexi replies.

The Dark Man hesitates again. Then he just shakes his head.

"You don't know?" asks Lexi.

"Right."

"You've never seen Viper?" Jake asks, incredulous.

"No."

"*Ever?*"

The Dark Man gestures at Marco. "Did you see him when you *worked* for him?"

Marco shakes his head no.

The Dark Man holds up his hands. "We've interviewed a good number of people who've had dealings with Viper," he says. "Some have heard his voice. None have seen him." He heaves a brooding sigh. "Our surveillance technology is the best in the world, and we can't even get a fuzzy telephoto shot or a police sketch."

Jake gestures around the HQ control room. "This is your surveillance center, right?"

"One of them, yes."

"So the Agency built this."

"Correct."

"Why did you abandon it?"

"That," states the Dark Man, "you most definitely do *not* wish to know."

This sends a chill up Jake's spine. "Is it safe here?" he asks.

"Actually, yes, it is," says the Dark Man. He turns to glance out the window. "These surrounding woods are really remarkably unpleasant, though."

"I have a question," Lucas says, raising his hand.

The Dark Man nods once at him.

"Why would you let a bunch of kids take over this unbelievably *sweet* place?" asks Lucas. He clears his throat.

"And, like . . . when are you planning to take it back?"

"We have no plans to reoccupy this post," says the Dark Man.

Lucas brightens. "Why not?"

Marco cracks a sardonic smile. "Because it's in better hands now," he says.

The Dark Man turns to Marco. "I wish that I could disagree with you." Then he points at Lucas. "It is true that you've used Stoneship most wisely, and your decryption and surveillance work has been surprisingly first-rate."

"What'd he say?" Lexi whispers to Lucas. "His voice box is too rumbly."

"He said we're good spies," answers Lucas.

Lexi nods. "That's so true," she says.

Then the Dark Man points at the console. "But it has also served our purpose to let the enemy think he succeeded in . . . eliminating us."

Lucas's mouth drops open. "Wait. Viper thinks you're *dead*?"

"Precisely."

"He hit you here, didn't he?" says Marco, peering down through the window again toward the cargo doors.

"No," says the Dark Man. His breath is unsteady for a second. Then he adds, "No. He drew us out. Nothing happened here."

Cyril sneezes again. "Hey, I'm not good, team," he says with droopy eyes. "I'm bad, in fact."

"Okay," says Marco. "Let's get this sick boy home."

The Dark Man nods. "I'll provide transport," he rumbles in his deep cyborg voice.

Lucas looks aghast. "Wait, you're a *stranger*," he says. "The moms of Carrolton would kill us!"

"Admirable prudence, Mr. Bixby," says the Dark Man. "But in fact, I'm no stranger. Believe me, I know you *far* better than I wish to." He looks over at Cyril. "Yes, let's get you home."

As Marco and the Dark Man move in tandem toward the floor hatch, Jake finds himself awed by their hulking size. Normally it would be comforting to have such large allies. But then he listens to the Dark Man's synthetic wheezing and thinks about nanite dust—tiny, relentless bits, hiding somewhere, waiting.

When you need a microscope to see your nemesis, things are very odd indeed.

9

GRAND THEFT AUTO

The next day. 12:03 p.m. Cat Horton slinks into the dark backstage area of the school auditorium. With feline stealth, she tiptoes to a power box, opens it, and pushes a button.

"Good evening, ladies and gentlemen," she whispers to herself.

Out front, the main curtain slowly slides open.

Cat smiles. "Welcome to the show," she says.

Next, Cat creeps catlike to a nearby door marked LIGHTING ACCESS and opens it. Quick as a cat, she scampers up the metal ladder inside, and just for the heck of it, I'm going to have her meow here a couple of times and then lick her paws.

The ladder leads up to, yes, a catwalk. (No, I'm not

making this up.[10]) This narrow metal walkway hangs from the ceiling over the auditorium stage. It gives the stage crew access to the stage lights and scenery lifts. It also gives you a pretty *sweet* overhead view of things.

At the top of the ladder, Cat stops. She listens carefully: Nothing. Then she slithers halfway across the catwalk to a spotlight hanging in a clamp from a metal ceiling track. She flips a switch on the unit—*click!* Six hundred watts of blazing, high-intensity white light shoot down at the stage below from the tungsten halogen lamp inside the metal housing. Then she pulls out a small crescent wrench.

With expert ease, Cat loosens the clamp with the wrench. Then she swivels the spotlight. She aims the beam out into the empty auditorium and tilts it up to a spot in the balcony.

"Perfect," she says.

Cat tightens the spotlight into position and clicks it off. Then she adjusts a Spy Link base unit attached to the belt of her jeans.

"Yo, Lexi, you hear me?" she murmurs.

She hears static in her earpiece, then a voice: Yeah, I'm here.

"Okay, girl, coast is clear," says Cat. "Time to do your monkey thing."

10. If I was making this up, it would be "fiction."

I'm coming in, over.

Cat hears a door crack open at the back of the theater. Just a few seconds later, Lexi's voice whispers in Cat's earpiece again: Okay, I'm up in the balcony.

"And testing Monkey spot . . . now," says Cat. She clicks on the spotlight.

Cat looks out across the auditorium. She sees Lexi in the balcony, illuminated in the spot, shading her eyes from the bright light. Lexi holds a small knapsack that looks heavy.

"Brilliant," Cat says.

She flicks off the light. Then she sits on the catwalk, directly over the center of the stage.

Now a new voice whispers in her earpiece: Calling Skyfox, this is Driver, do you read me? Over. Repeat, this is Driver, do you copy, Skyfox? Over.

Cat rolls her eyes. "I hear you, soldier."

Roger, replies Lucas. He speaks very slowly. Has Monkey completed her phase one deployment? Repeat, has Monkey—?

"Please," Cat interrupts. "Lexi, can you see the ledge I told you about?"

It's dark, but I see it. Lexi's voice is excited and electric.

"And the curtain?"

I see everything, says Lexi. And I'm ready.

* * *

Lucas Bixby sits in pitch-black darkness.

He's inside a maintenance closet in the gym—the only place in school he can find privacy. "Roger-roger on that, Skyfox and Monkey," he says. Then: "Ow! Hold the channel, please."

What? asks Cat.

"Uh, just . . . hang on a sec," says Lucas.

He digs in his pocket and pulls out a tiny Micro Ear Light, which he turns on and hooks over his left ear for hands-free, head-directed lighting. Turning his head to cast the red glow to his left, Lucas sees a row of industrial dust mops and a big bucket of dry sponges. A squeegee handle juts from the bucket too . . . right into his ribs.

You okay there, Lima Bob? asks Cat.

"That's Lima *Bravo.*" Lucas pushes away the squeegee handle and adds, "Over."

There is a long pause. Finally Cat says, **Are we waiting for something?**

"I'm holding for your reply," says Lucas.

Well, don't.

"Excellent, then let's get a report from Recon Badger," says Lucas quickly. "Recon Badger, this is Lima Bravo, do we have Tango Delta on the move yet? Over."

Static crackles over the Spy Link channel for a few empty seconds.

Who's Recon Badger? asks Lexi.

I forgot, says Cat.

Lexi says, Jake is Hedgehog, right?

"There is no Hedgehog!" exclaims Lucas, exasperated.

No, no, I'm Recon Badger, sorry, Jake's voice reports over the channel. Dude, it's the Tango Delta that's really got me stumped.

"That's the *target duffel*," says Lucas. "Tango Delta. Target duffel." He sighs. "Really, people, I need better focus from you at the tactical mission briefings."

Whatever, says Cat. Look, we're all set here. What's going on outside, Bixby?

Out on the playground, Jake Bixby slouches with fake casual cool near a door leading into the auditorium lobby. It's warmer today, so kids run around the school yard shrieking, falling, beating large rocks together, and burbling in the usual lunchtime manner.

Jake misses Cyril, who lies in bed at home, recovering from the flu. Jake wears his Spy Link headset, but he also has a Micro Agent Listener hooked on his left ear. He faces across the playground to aim the listening device at Brill, Wilson, and a large cadre of Wolf Pack minions who snuffle and bark and whine near the fence. Jake can make out bits of conversation via the Listener, especially Brill's loud, baying voice.

"No movement yet from Brill and the pack," reports Jake. "So far they're just telling vile, disgusting jokes and making depraved comments. Say, would you like to hear some of them?"

I'd rather chew a wad of aluminum foil, says Cat over the Spy Link.

Does Brill have his duffel bag? Lucas asks anxiously.

"Oh, yeah," says Jake.

You're sure it's the same one? asks Lucas.

"Almost positive," says Jake.

Almost? repeats Lucas.

"I'm pretty sure it's the one you described," says Jake.

You're pretty sure?

"Okay, okay, give me a second to verify," says Jake. He pulls out a pair of powerful Spy Vision binoculars and trains them on a duffel bag near Brill's feet. "Okay, what specifically am I looking for here, Lima Bravo?"

You want a blue Trail Blazer gym bag with sturdy nylon construction, a sporty white stripe, two mesh-trimmed gusset pockets, a padded grab handle, and, of course, the striking bicolor TB logo design.

Jake nods. "Did some Internet market research, eh?"

I want that car back, Jake.

Jake adjusts the focus. "Yep, that's it," he says.

As Jake gazes through the binoculars at the Wolf Pack, he notices some fuzzy movement in the background, out of focus beyond the fence. He adjusts the binoculars to refocus on the spot across Ridgeview Drive, right at the edge of Stoneship Woods.

There, a low stand of bushes is rocking wildly. Then it stops.

Jake keeps the binoculars trained on the spot. For a few seconds nothing moves.

Then a large black creature darts from the bush into the tree line.

"What the—?" says Jake.

He tries to locate the animal in the trees, but it moves so fast he can't keep his scope on it.

"All units, all units, I've marked a large black animal, moving along the perimeter of Stoneship Woods!" Jake says breathlessly.

Whoa! replies Lucas. **Is it a dog? Maybe it's the nanoswarm in the shape of the black dog again!**

"It could be, I guess," says Jake. "But to be honest, it didn't look like a dog."

What did it look like? Lucas asks.

"Let me try to find it again!" says Jake, panning the binoculars left. He sees no movement now. He pans back to the right . . . and suddenly finds himself looking right into the giant scrunge-mutant face of Brill Joseph.

"Aaaaaaggghh!" Jake screams.

He lowers the scope to see Brill and the Wolf Pack moving swiftly in his direction. They're still about twenty yards away, but the binoculars have magnified Brill's face to foul, beastly proportions. Brill still lugs the duffel bag.

"Whew!" says Jake, sliding sideways from the lobby door. "Okay, team, Tango Delta is on the move. Cat, Lexi, they should be there in sixty seconds. Recommend radio silence."

Okay, says Cat. Skyfox out.

Monkey out, Lexi says.

Jake says, "Are you ready, Driver?"

Heads-up unit is mounted, says Lucas eagerly. Time to roll.

A minute later Cat stares down at Brill, who stands in the middle of the stage directly below the catwalk. Wolf Pack minions form a loose circle around him. Brill sets his duffel bag on the ground, opens it, and takes out the Spy Video Car. Then he sets it on the ground.

Wilson Wills, the Wolf Pack second-in-command, steps up to Brill. "I still don't get it, dude," he says. "Why here, on the stage?"

"How the [censored] do I know?" Brill blusters.

"Read the note again," says Wilson.

Brill curses again and digs his hand into one of his cargo pants pockets. He pulls out a crumpled piece of paper.

"You read it," he says, handing it to Wilson.

Wilson holds up the paper and reads, "'The Magic Car can be activated *only* in the center of the auditorium stage.'" Wilson frowns and looks around. "And it's signed, *Lupine Larry*."

Above, Cat struggles to suppress a snort of laughter.

"Okay," Brill says. "Now what?"

Everybody stares at the car.

Suddenly it moves forward a few inches, then stops.

"Oooooooooohh!" says the Wolf Pack.

The car turns in a quick circle.

"Aaaaaaaahhh!" says the Wolf Pack.

Brill quickly picks up the vehicle and holds it close to his face, examining it.

I'm looking right up his nose! gasps Lucas over the Spy Link. My God, I've never seen such putrescent nasal mucus.

I'm ready, Lexi whispers.

Cool, says Lucas. Wait until he puts the car back down.

Cat leans farther over the catwalk railing, watching carefully. Then she quietly stands and puts her hand on the spotlight switch.

Below, Brill shakes the car and listens to it. Then he sets it back on the stage floor. It sits there, unmoving. He nudges it with his foot.

"Stupid car!" he says. "Now it won't go!" He gives it a kick. "This thing is stupid!"

The car zooms in a quick circle around Brill's feet. The Wolf Pack starts laughing loudly. *"Haargh hargh hargh, hargh haaargh!"*

"Okay, Lexi," whispers Cat into her Spy Link. "Now!"

As Brill spins around, following the Spy Video Car's

movement, a splash of water suddenly explodes on his back. He jerks around with an evil glare. "Who did that?" he yells.

Another water explosion on his leg makes him jump and scream.

"Water balloons!" shouts Wilson.

Water-filled balloons start bombarding the stage, one after another. Brill, Wilson, and the pack members start howling and running around mindlessly. Brill tries to gaze out into the auditorium, but another balloon splats on his shoes.

"Okay, Monkey," says Cat quietly. "Show yourself."

She clicks the spotlight on. From the balcony, the illuminated Lexi waves down at the Wolf Pack.

"Guys!" she yells. "Up here!"

All lupine eyes snap in the direction of her voice.

"Lopez, are you whacked?" snarls Brill.

Lexi can't help it. She starts hooting with laughter.

"Wow," whispers Cat in admiration. "That's a *huge* laugh. Very impressive indeed."

Cat quickly loosens the light fixture clamp with her wrench again.

Meanwhile, Lexi hurls her last few water bombs. *Splat!* *Splat!* The balloons are small, the size of tangerines, and thus perfect for throwing.

"*Mangle her!*" shrieks Brill.

He and Wilson lead a howling charge down the

stage's side stairs into the auditorium. From there they veer up the side aisle toward the balcony staircase. Back up on the catwalk, Cat swivels the spotlight slightly, aiming the beam at a small ledge just above a side exit door.

"Okay, Lexi girl, there's your target," she says into the Spy Link. She glances down at the abandoned Spy Video Car directly below her on the stage floor. "And Driver, you are now free and clear to exit, fast and furious."

Across the auditorium, Lexi climbs up onto the balcony railing.

Hey, this seems like a perfectly good time to cut away from the auditorium.

Yeah, let's go back to the broom closet, where Lucas jams a remote control joystick forward. He stares hard into the eyepiece on his headset, watching the live feed as the Spy Video Car accelerates across the stage.

"Recon Badger, Recon Badger, are you in position? Over." he calls loudly.

Ready, bro, answers Jake via the Spy Link.

"Let's bring baby home," says Lucas.

There is a pause. Then: **Uh-oh,** says Jake. **Cat, it's locked.**

What's locked? Cat asks urgently over the link.

The backstage door, says Jake. **It won't open.**

"What?" shouts Lucas, leaping to his feet in the closet.

This sets off a cataclysmic chain reaction. As he stands, Lucas kicks the bucket. No, he doesn't *die*—instead, he literally kicks the sponge-filled bucket, which slams into the row of mops. This awakens the mops, which shake their tendrils and then fall angrily onto Lucas. The mop attack knocks the Micro Ear Light off his ear, plunging the closet interior back into pure horrific darkness.

You're mop meat now, Bixby! hisses one mop close to his ear.

No more kid vomit to mop up! hisses another. *Not from you, anyway!*

The mops crawl all over Lucas, moaning and entwining their clammy mop strands around his face and arms. Okay, so maybe they're just falling. But they seem alive to Lucas, so shut up.

"Aaaaaaaahh!" Lucas screams. "Help!"

Swatting at mops, he falls. Unfortunately, he lands directly atop the Spy Video Car's remote controller. This jams both the steering and the acceleration joysticks hard in one direction.

In his eyepiece, Lucas sees the live action feed as the vehicle swerves and speeds directly toward the vast, dark maw of the orchestra pit.

"*Nooooooo!*" he screams.

* * *

Meanwhile, Lexi takes a deep breath, smiles, and leaps from the balcony railing. She lands with soft grace on the narrow ledge above the exit door.

Behind her, Brill arrives at the balcony railing.

"She jumped!" he bellows.

Lexi gazes up at him. "Wow, look, Brill. I'm down here now," she says.

"Get her!" howls Brill.

As the Wolf Pack shrieks and reverses its direction, Lexi grabs a pleat of the nearby acoustic wall curtain and gracefully slides down to the floor. As she sprints to the stage, she glances over to see the Spy Video Car shoot off the stage into the orchestra pit . . . and hears Lucas's anguished cries in her earpiece.

"Who's attacking you?" she asks.

Mops! screams Lucas via Spy Link. **Mops!**

"Mops?"

Mops!

Cat scampers out from backstage to meet Lexi. "Crap!" she says. "The car fell into the pit."

Lexi peers down into the pit's darkness. "Can we get down there?" she asks.

"Not from here," says Cat. "Follow me! Quick!"

Cat! yells Jake over the channel. **The door's still locked.**

"We'll open it from the inside," Cat says as she sprints ahead of Lexi into the backstage area. She can hear the snarling of the Wolf Pack out front, getting closer. "Lucas! How's the car?"

Holy cow! shouts Lucas happily. It landed on its wheels! I'm driving it again. It survived the fall! I can see a lighted hall up ahead.

"What about the mops?" cries Lexi as she runs.

It's okay, Lucas says. I killed them.

"You killed the mops?"

I strangled them with my bare hands.

"Lucas, there's a corridor that leads from the orchestra pit right to the band rehearsal room," says Cat breathlessly. "That must be the lighted hall you see! Drive the car out and park it under the rehearsal bandstand, and then I'll run downstairs and nab it."

The girls reach the backstage door. Cat grabs the handle and yanks hard.

The Wolf Pack is closing in!

Wow, this is getting stressful.

Back in the broom closet, Lucas tries to steer the Spy Video Car out of the pit labyrinth. The exit corridor curves around corner after corner, left, then right, then right, then left.

"This is nuts!" Lucas shouts. "Who designed this? The Phantom of the Opera?"

Music people are weird, pants Cat over the Spy Link. Hey! What the—? I can't open the door either!

How could the door be locked from both sides? asks Jake.

Dang, somebody key-locked the dead bolt! says Cat. Some teacher must have locked it after I got inside.

Meanwhile, Lucas guides the spy car around one last corner . . . and comes up against a closed door.

Lucas groans. "Great flying monkeys!" he cries out. "Cat, there's a closed door. Could anything else *possibly* go wrong?"

Suddenly the closet door flies open.

"Who's in here?" growls an ominous voice.

Squinting in the sudden light of day, Lucas finds himself staring into the surprised face of Coach Volpe. Coach Volpe is the school janitor, who also doubles as the phys ed instructor. His PE classes usually consist of broom races down the hallways or toilet-plunging contests in the lavatories.

"Bixby, what are you doing in here?" asks Coach.

"Hey, Coach Volpe," says Lucas. "Well, I'm, heh heh, I'm, I'm. Heh." He slides the video headset off his face. "Actually, I have no explanation whatsoever, sir. None. I cannot even remotely explain my presence in this broom closet."

Coach Volpe grins. It's a hideous, yellow grin.

"You're playing one of those VR videogames, aren't you?" says Coach, pointing at the headset.

Lucas looks down at the headset in his hands.

"Huh," he says. "Yes. Yes, Coach, that is so *exactly* what

I'm doing." He holds up the headset. "It's, uh, a driving game."

"Hand it over," Coach Volpe orders.

Lucas feels panic. But then he raises his eyebrows.

"Sure, here, Coach," he says, holding out the headset with a big smile. "Say, you wanna take it for a quick spin? I'll, like, give you instructions."

Coach Volpe looks down at the headset.

Then he cracks another hideous grin.

Cat and Lexi stare at the backstage door.

"Trapped!" says Lexi. "Sheesh!"

Cat turns with a determined face toward the stage and steps forward into a karate stance, ready to defend as the howling of the Wolf Pack grows closer. But then she gets an idea.

"Quick! Over here!" she whispers.

Cat leads Lexi into the darkness behind a nearby door that stands in a frame with nothing around it—a fake stage door. It's made of solid, heavy wood. Cat quickly opens the door . . . and then pulls it shut hard with a loud *slam!*

Two seconds later Brill and pack burst through the curtains into the unlit backstage area. "Did you hear that door slam?" cries Brill. "They got away!" Wolves trip over cords and cables in the darkness; bodies hit the ground left and right.

"Halt!" Brill orders. "You [censored] losers. Where's the door?"

"Over there." A minion points.

As his eyes adjust, Brill feels his way to the backstage door and gives the handle a yank. "Locked!" he says. He looks around. As his eyes adjust, he sees the fake door frame nearby.

"What's that?" he asks, pointing.

A dozen pairs of lupine eyes turn to look.

Both Cat and Lexi are frozen in a crouch behind the frame, ready to run. But then they hear Jake's voice via Spy Link.

Hang tight, gals, he says. **Solution coming.**

Brill takes a menacing step toward the door frame, and his pack follows. Suddenly they all hear the sound of a key jiggling in the dead-bolt lock behind them.

The pack turns to the backstage door.

It swings open to reveal the gruesome silhouette of a large, frightening woman.

Jake Bixby stands next to her, saying, "Thanks a million, Mrs. Burnskid. I know my Math Difficulties book is in here somewhere, and without it I'd be lost, really lost in life, pretty much."

The hulking shadow-colossus takes one step through the doorway. "No one is allowed *unsupervised* in here," she hisses like a Death Harpy.

The Wolf Pack screams.

Jake backs away, knowing the carnage could last hours.

Now Jake sprints hard to the north staircase and leaps down many stairs at a time, a dangerous stunt that children should never attempt unless guard dogs or lethal security laserbots are chasing you.

Jake, of course, has been listening to everything on the Spy Link, including Lucas's encounter with Coach Volpe down in the gym area.

"I'm on the way down," he gasps as he leaps down another flight of stairs. "Okay, I'm entering the Music area . . . entering the band rehearsal room."

Mercifully, the band room is empty. Jake looks around quickly and spots several doors. All of them are faculty offices . . . except one, a white door.

Over the Spy Link, Jake hears Lucas give "videogame control instructions" to Coach Volpe. He hurries to the white door, which has a small plaque nailed to it that reads ORCHESTRA PIT ENTRANCE.

"I've found it," he says. "Lucas, I'm opening the door now."

Go for it, Coach! says Lucas with forced enthusiasm. **You're in a maze and, and, uh, you have to find the open maze door to escape the Horrible Throbbing Luctors of Empheysium.**

Jake yanks the door open and sees the Spy Video Car just as it slams into a wall.

At that moment Lucas drags a squeegee across a dripping office window in the gym complex.

"Keep scrubbing there, Bixby," says Coach Volpe, wearing the video headset and jabbing at the control joysticks with his huge opposable thumbs. "You've earned at least a triple-window punishment for bringing this contraband electronic device onto school property." He grimaces. "*Dang it!* I hit another wall."

Lucas, I'm ready, says Jake via Spy Link.

"Okay," replies Lucas. He looks over at the coach. "Uh, okay. Do you see the door yet?"

Coach Volpe's tongue sneaks out of his mouth as he tries to steer the car. After a few seconds, his eyes grow big.

"Yes, there's the door," he says. "It's open. But what the *heck* is that in the doorway?"

"That would be . . . the Guardian," says Lucas. "Yes. The Minotaur of the Maze."

"Minotaur?" Coach Volpe sounds suspicious. "It looks like a kid in a baseball cap."

"Yes, well, I customized the Guardian boss-monster in the Custom Monster Builder software," says Lucas quickly. "I'll bet the foul beast looks kind of familiar, doesn't it?"

"I'll say!" says Coach. "It looks like my mom!"

Lucas snorts. "The Minotaur looks like your mom?"

And what a handsome woman she is, Jake says flatly.

"That really doesn't look like a Minotaur," insists Coach Volpe.

"Again, it's a *custom* Minotaur," says Lucas. "Okay, now, when you get close, be sure to dodge to the left. *The left!*" Lucas speaks slowly, as if to a small child. "Got it, Coach? *Dodge to the left.* That would be the monster's *right*, if, say, you were seeing things through the eyes of the monster."

Dude, you're busting my ears, says Jake with a hint of amusement. **Got it. He's going to my right.**

"I got it, I got it," cries Coach Volpe, glancing over at Lucas. "Say, you missed that lower left pane, son. And here I go!"

Coach Volpe accelerates the Spy Video Car forward. As it approaches the "Minotaur Guardian" in the view screen, Coach yanks the steering joystick to the left. Suddenly he sees the camera view rise up, flip downward, and then dive into a black hole.

Got it! calls Jake over the Spy Link.

"The monster got me!" Coach Volpe screams. He jabs at the controls. "Hey, everything went black!"

"Oh, no," says Lucas. "That confounded game must have *crashed* again."

Looking disappointed, Coach Volpe removes the headset and puts it down. "Put this gadget in your locker, son," he says. "If I see it out again, I'll be forced to confiscate it."

"Yes, sir!" Lucas answers, fighting the urge to salute.

Baby is coming home to papa, says Jake in Lucas's ear. **Recon Badger, out.**

Grinning, Lucas gives the office window an extra bit of polish.

UP THE CREEK

Friday, February 1. 4:34 p.m. Lexi Lopez slaps a killer shot on goal. The ball skips under the goalie's extended stick.

"Score!" Lexi shouts, raising her arms.

"Pure luck," calls the goalie, Justin Bolby. Justin has been Team Spy Gear's netminder, and he does a darn good job, considering.

Q: *Considering what?*

A: Considering the fact that he's wretchedly bad.

Fortunately, the stellar defensive work of the Bixby brothers has kept Justin from seeing very many shots this season.

Team Spy Gear is just wrapping up its final practice before tomorrow's big broomball game against the Wolf Pack. Nearby, just off the ice, Lucas holds a cell phone to his ear. Jake stands next to him.

"Still no answer," says Lucas, listening.

"Leave another message," Jake suggests.

"Dude, I've left, like, three already," says Lucas. "And I designated each one Priority Alpha."

"You sure that's the correct cell number?" asks Jake anxiously. "Maybe Marco changed it . . . you know, for security reasons."

"It's Marco's voice leaving the away message," says Lucas, flipping his phone shut. "So I'm sure it's right."

"Hmmm," murmurs Jake. "This is . . . not good."

"Plus, what's up with *this* thing?" Lucas says. He pulls the Omega Link out of his backpack. He looks at it. "Two measly one-word clues so far." Then he shakes it a little and looks again. "Help us out here, big guy," he says to the device.

"Maybe everyone at the Agency is still sick," says Jake.

"I guess we're supposed to figure out everything by ourselves now," says Lucas. He jams the Omega Link into the backpack again. "Maybe we should pay another visit to Blackwater Estate."

Jake glances south toward Stoneship Woods. The wind is dead and the trees are deathly quiet.

"What's going *on* out there?" he says quietly.

Lexi jogs up to them from the ice. She looks exhilarated. "Brill's boys are going down," she says. "We're, like, *so* good."

Lucas raises his stick. He and Lexi do the clacking stick thing: *Clack! Clack! Clack!*

"I love being eleven," says Lexi.

Jake nods. "Yes, those were the days." He sighs.

Suddenly Jake's cell phone rings. He flips it open, looks at the incoming number, and brightens. He holds the phone to his ear.

"Yo, sick boy," he says.

As Jake listens, his face grows serious. Then he says, "Got it!" and flips the phone shut. He gives Lucas and Lexi an uncertain look.

"Cyril wants all units on the Spy Link channel," he informs them. "He's got news."

Cyril sits at the computer desk in his bedroom, surrounded by John Coltrane posters, hockey paraphernalia, and stacks of jazz CDs. A huge pink blanket is wrapped around his shoulders. He finishes hooking a Spy Link headset to his ear.

"Everybody on?" he asks. "Hello? Hello?"

Jake here, says Jake over the link.

Lima Bravo, I copy you, over, says Lucas.

I'm on, says Lexi.

"Excellent, folks," says Cyril. "Welcome to my illness, and let's get right to business, shall we?" His skinny arms suddenly explode from the pink swirls of the blanket, not unlike aliens bursting from a body, except not all bloody and gruesome, plus there are fingers at the end instead of razor-tusks. Aside from that, it's *exactly* the same. Speaking of fingers, Cyril's fingers start clacking away at his computer keyboard and he says, "Hey, let's start with a little online map fun!"

Jake says, Okay?

"Well, now," continues Cyril, still typing. "Remember that local nanotechnology company, the one based in Carrolton?"

Yeah, it was called, uh . . . INS, says Lucas.

"Ding!" says Cyril. "Intelligent NanoSystems. Well done, Lima Bravo. Next time I see you, I'm going to give you a fish."

After a short pause, Lucas says, Thanks.

"But you have to bark like a seal," says Cyril.

Why? asks Lucas.

"For extra points," Cyril explains. "Now, as you may recall, the corporate address listed on the INS website was 3000 Lakeshore Drive. So just for fun, because I've been bored to the point of drooling insanity here in my sad, wretched little sickroom, I tried doing a map search. And guess what?"

What? reply Jake, Lucas, and Lexi at the exact same time.

"Technically, there *is* no 3000 Lakeshore Drive," says Cyril.

What do you mean, technically? Jake asks.

"Technically, the last address on Lakeshore Drive is 2900. That property is right at the corner of Lakeshore and Agincourt, where Lakeshore Drive ends. But guess what?"

What? reply Jake, Lucas, and Lexi at the exact same time.

"If you continue north across Agincourt Drive from where Lakeshore Drive ends, guess what's directly across the street?" asks Cyril.

There is a pause. Then at the exact same time, Jake, Lucas, and Lexi reply, **What?**

"The entrance to Blackwater Estate," he says.

Okay, I put a space break there just for effect.

Feel free to insert your own scary music—maybe a bunch of violins going *Reeeek! Reeeek! Reeeek!* really fast and scratchy.

"So if there was an actual 3000 Lakeshore Drive," Cyril explains, "it would be Blackwater House. Again, technically, the estate address is listed on Agincourt— 10001 Agincourt Drive, to be exact. But isn't this a little too ripe to be just coincidence?"

Wow! says Jake. **Well done, Mister Spy Guy.**

I knew there was something about that place, says Lucas. **Nice job, Cyril.**

"I appreciate it, guys. I love glory, as you know. But there's more."

More?

"More."

How much more?

"Way more." Cyril taps the Enter key. "Between ago-nized fits of coughing, I did some additional research on nano-stuff. Let me pass along some of the more interest-ing data nuggets that I mined."

He looks at an onscreen Web page on his monitor. Across the top of the page is a title: "The Gray Goo Problem."

"I did a search on ecophagy and found a site entirely devoted to this gray goo doomsday scenario that Marco described—you know, where self-replicating nanorobots go berserk and eat up the entire planet's biomass," con-tinues Cyril. "One of the articles is by a dude at MIT who says that the possibility of a gray goo scenario is *vastly* overrated. And get this: He says that *viruses* are actually the most perfect examples of self-replicating nanolife anyone could possibly imagine. Yet after more than four billion years of evolution, viruses have not gobbled up the world and turned us all into gray goo. Given this fact, it seems highly unlikely that some manmade technodust could manage to do so."

So he's saying, don't worry about ecophagy? asks Lucas.

"Ah, another fish for Lima Bravo!" says Cyril. "And here's a little tidbit I found that might explain why the swarm ran away from my sneezing at Stoneship HQ the other day."

It's the flu, guesses Jake.

"You crazy barking Bixbys," says Cyril, clicking open another page. "Yes, exactly. This Nobel-honcho in England suggests that if a nanomachine is made of basic organic molecules—the most likely composition—then it might find itself vulnerable to assault by bacteria, viruses, yeasts, fungi, or other micro life-forms." Cyril starts speaking in a stuffy English accent. "At the very least the little bugger may find itself unable to *process* such an attack. Indeed, the very presence of an aggressive microbial life-form may *befuddle* the robotic minibeast, disrupting its programming or even shutting down its functions."

Wow again! says Jake. So to translate, maybe the flu viruses flying out of your nose, like, freaked out the nanites?

"That certainly seems like a possibility," agrees Cyril. "And here's one last note of interest. A laboratory study of various biovore nanostructures at Caltech showed that nanoswarms could be remarkably resistant to certain kinds of physical disruption—air movement, like wind, for example. But lab nanites showed a vulnerability to sound-wave disruption."

Cyril smiles, big.

"In other words," he concludes, "loud sounds can mess up certain kinds of nanoswarms."

* * *

As Jake listens to Cyril, he notices a blue car moving very slowly between the Bald Spot and Stoneship Woods on Ridgeview Drive. He thinks, *That's Mr. Latimer.* Then he wonders, *Why is he driving so slow?*

A second later Jake sees the answer to his question.

"Look," he says, pointing. "Mr. Latimer is following some squirrels."

Yes, the blue Toyota Avalon trolls along beside three large squirrels hopping through the open space just east of the Bald Spot rinks. Lucas stares at the animals, then notices movement farther up the road to his right, near Blackwater Creek.

"A snow devil!" he whispers. He points to the overpass where Ridgeview Drive crosses the creek. "You can just see the top of it."

Indeed, the white whirlwind appears to be peeking over the top of the embankment next to the bridge.

"Hey, two more just popped out," says Lexi, gazing across the road at Stoneship Woods. "See? They're coming out of the trees."

Two small snow devils pulse up and down, right out in the open, as they move toward Ridgeview Drive. Then they drift slowly west along the road toward the creek. Each one is no more than two feet high. This duo joins up with the lone whirlwind by the bridge embankment.

"They're so tiny," Lexi says. "They look almost . . . cute."

"They're spying on us," says Lucas darkly.

"Cyril," reports Jake. "We've got three, repeat, three nanoswarms, casing out the Bald Spot. Any recommendations? Over."

Yeah, Cyril suggests. Go yell at them.

"Really?" says Jake.

It's worth a try, says Cyril. They're small, right?

"Yeah, they're little fellows," says Jake, glancing toward the creek.

Give it a shot, urges Cyril. He clears his throat. Yell really loud, he adds.

"Okay," says Jake. "Let's go." He starts walking toward the creek.

"Wait," says Lucas. "If sonic waves really work to disperse these things, I've got a better idea."

Lucas heads toward Ridgeview Drive, where the blue Toyota still creeps slowly down the road. Jake and Lexi follow. When Lucas reaches the snow-packed street, he flags down Mr. Latimer.

The car pulls up and the passenger-side window rolls down.

"Hey, Lucas," calls Mr. Latimer. "What's doing?"

Lucas approaches the window. "Hi, Mr. Latimer," he says. "Say, do you still have that air horn you always use at the Carrolton High School football games? You know, the one that really annoys everybody?"

Mr. Latimer frowns. "That's an odd question."

"Yes," says Lucas. "It's a question that really comes right out of the blue, doesn't it?"

"Hmmm, I think I have it here," Mr. Latimer says. "But why?"

"I need something that makes a really loud noise," Lucas explains, glancing at the author. "And apparently *someone* couldn't come up with anything better than this ridiculous plot device."

"I understand," says Mr. Latimer. He unhooks his safety belt and starts digging through items in the backseat. Then he turns to the passenger window, holding out an aluminum canister with a plastic red horn attached to the top. "This is a classic Fieldhouse model," he says. "Careful, though. It puts out a deafening, one-hundred-twenty-decibel blast of sound."

"Excellent!" says Lucas. "This is perfect. Thanks."

Mr. Latimer turns to gaze out into the open field to the north. He frowns again.

"Hey, what happened to my squirrels?" he asks. "They disappeared."

The three kids look too. The squirrel trio is nowhere to be seen. However, another small white whirlwind drifts across the road up ahead of the Toyota. It stops in the road for a second, pulsing up and down. Then it abruptly darts down the creek bank.

"Let's go!" shouts Jake.

"Thanks again, Mr. Latimer," calls Lucas as he wields the air horn and sprints after the snow devil.

"Sure," Mr. Latimer replies. "You kids have fun." Then he adds to himself, "I guess I'll just . . . sit here and wait for those squirrels to reappear." He gives the author a disdainful look.

The three kids sprint across the road. By the time they reach the creek bank, the four snow devils have disappeared.

"Careful!" warns Lucas, examining the ground. "They might have collapsed right here, under our feet. They could suddenly rise up anywhere."

"No, there they are!" Lexi cries. "They're running up the creek!"

All four whirlwinds float over the creek ice, moving slowly south into Stoneship Woods. With Jake leading the way, the kids bound down the snowy bank and start running upstream along the creek's edge.

The chase goes on for several minutes. Up ahead, the snow devils dart erratically from one side of the creek to the other. Every time the kids get close, the four spinners zip further upstream.

Finally Jake slows to a halt, heaving vapor into the dusky air. He puts his hands on his knees.

"I don't think we can catch them," he gasps.

"Yeah, and it's getting darker," says Lucas, looking

up through the trees at the leaden gray sky.

Jake, panting down toward the snow at his feet, suddenly notices a set of tracks. Each three-toed print tapers to a long, sharp point.

"Holy rice cakes!" he exclaims. "What the heck made these?"

Lucas looks down. His expression turns grave. "Those are some *big* claws there."

"Is it a bear or something?" asks Lexi nervously.

Jake shakes his head. "No, bear tracks are more rounded, and usually show five distinct toe pads. These are just . . . very freaky."

The Bixbys have been hiking through forests for as long as Jake can remember. Long ago, Mrs. Bixby, his mother, prepared a 146-page "Hiker's Guide" for family study. Every Bixby family hike is preceded by a sixty-question pop quiz, including an animal tracks recognition section. Jake and Lucas have both memorized the tracks of every large mammal known to the continent, including the West Indian manatee and the North American hog-nosed skunk.

But neither boy recognizes these three-toed tracks in the snow.

And that's when they hear the low, throaty growl. It comes from foliage somewhere behind them. And it's close. The three kids turn to face the sound.

Jake immediately puts a hand on each kid's shoulder.

"Don't panic," he says quietly.

"What do we do?" asks Lexi tightly.

"Just back up slowly," Jake tells them. "Don't run. Keep facing the sound."

Hey, what's going on, guys? blares Cyril's voice over the Spy Link. **What sound?**

The growl continues. Punctuated by snorts, it grows louder.

Guys? calls Cyril.

"Keep backing away," says Jake calmly.

Inside, he is anything but calm. But both Bixbys know what to do when confronted by a large, growling mammal:

1. Keep calm.

2. Face the animal, but avoid direct eye contact.

3. Back away *slowly* while talking in a calm, authoritative manner.

4. If the animal tries to attack, react aggressively by shouting, waving your arms, and throwing rocks or sticks.

5. Change your automotive oil every three thousand miles, unless you don't have a car.

Jake notices a shrub rustling where the growl is coming from. He keeps a hand on each younger kid's shoulder as the three back up.

Lucas holds up Mr. Latimer's air horn, ready to blast.

Lexi breathes deeply, her eyes bright with both fear and thrill.

The kids back around a gang of ragged, mean-looking cottonwood saplings into a creekside clearing. The snarling is steady now; Jake sees a flash of red eyes. They gleam in the gathering darkness.

Something about them is familiar.

"Cyril, do you hear me?" he says quietly. "Buddy, you might want to put in a 911 call for us. We're just a couple hundred yards down Blackwater Creek from the north end of the woods."

Roger that, says Cyril quickly. **Actually, I'm sending in something better than 911. Hang tight, kids.**

Jake, Lucas, and Lexi back into the clearing. Behind them they suddenly hear a strange sound. It starts as a cross between humming, buzzing, and hissing. But as they turn their heads to look, the sound deepens into a low, throbbing drone.

There, rising up in a column thirty feet high, is a huge, black whirlwind.

(11)

NIGHT MOVES

Jake stares in awe at the towering column of black dust. Its low, throbbing vibration rises to a roar, and several smaller twisters sprout like black tentacles from the central vortex.

"Cyril," he croaks. "We've got a Category F5 swarm out here. Very large." He tries to swallow. "Very scary."

I can hear it, says Cyril bleakly.

Bixby! calls another voice over the channel—a deeper voice. Listen carefully, and do exactly as I say!

"Dark Man!" Jake exclaims.

Help is on the way, says the Dark Man. But you must distract the swarm for another few minutes.

"Another *few minutes?*" gulps Lucas.

Lexi gazes up into the menacing black mass of the nanobeast. She can feel its bass reverb in the pit of her stomach.

"Will it eat us?" she asks.

No, Miss Lopez, says the Dark Man. **Not if you follow my instructions.**

One of the tentacles reaches out toward Lexi. She screams and throws up her hands. Instinctively, Lucas jumps forward and unleashes a blast from his air horn. The black tentacle retracts.

"Ha!" shouts Lucas. "It works!"

But then three more feelers burst out of the entity. Lucas fires more air-horn blasts, but the dust appendages whip around him quickly, approaching from different angles with stunning speed.

"Help!" shouts Lucas.

"Talk to us," Jake says into the Spy Link. "Quickly!"

Confuse it! barks the Dark Man. **The swarm thinks it knows your behavior. Give it something truly abnormal to ponder.**

"But Cyril's not here!" says Lexi.

Move around each other. Circle and weave!

Jake immediately runs in a circle around Lucas. As he does, one of the dust tentacles curls back cautiously. Jake waves his arms wildly. It backs away farther.

Lucas spins to face Lexi.

"Dude!" he yells. "Go totally monkey girl on it!"

Lexi's eyes widen. Then she starts spinning in a pirouette, arms out. She tucks her arms and tightens the rotation, gaining speed. She abruptly breaks out of the spin and does a few perfect cartwheels around the boys, then adds a couple of backflips.[11]

The massive black dust tower roils and pulsates with glints of silver, processing this new Lexi data. Its "voice"— the deep reverberating roar—lowers deeper still to a rumble, as if the beast were thinking.

"Keep it up, kid!" shouts Jake.

But then, in a flash, the huge swarm descends on them. It moves so fast they barely see the maneuver. All three kids start coughing, and they flail wildly at the black, choking dust that hisses around them.

"I can't see!" Lexi shrieks.

"Dark Man," gasps Jake. "It's not working. It's all over us." He falls to his knees, hacking nanodust from his throat.

Lucas, dude, use that air horn! calls Cyril over the Spy Link.

Lucas tries to respond but his mouth is caked, and all he can get out is a squawk. But he wields his air horn. First he shoots sound blasts in random directions. Then he just holds down the trigger, waving the blaring horn wildly around his head.

This works briefly. The horn blasts seem to tear big holes in the nanobeast, and it twirls away to regroup. Slowly, the ragged gaps in its shape fill back in. As it

11. As all Spy Gear fans know, Lexi Lopez has been taking both ballet and gymnastics lessons since shortly before she was born.

reshapes, the entity rears up, rising even higher—forty, maybe fifty feet tall now, a huge, hissing, hostile shape. It seems ready to renew its attack.

But then Jake hears an earsplitting howl somewhere behind him.

A large, dark creature springs over him and wades into the heart of the swarm.

"What is *that*?" Lucas gasps. His voice is barely more than a scratchy whisper. "What's it doing?"

Lexi wipes at her stinging eyes. Black tears stream down her cheeks, but she squints to see the animal. "It's fighting the swarm," she says. "It's protecting us!"

The creature is hard to see as the swarm encircles it and the late-afternoon dusk deepens. But its howls and screeches are piercing, literally—the sounds tear hole after hole in the nanobot entity.

What's happening? asks the Dark Man via Spy Link. Reports, please!

Jake scrambles to his feet, grabs the two younger kids, and pulls them away from the wild fight. "There's an animal, a black animal," he reports quickly. "It jumped into the swarm. They're fighting!" Jake backs away, staring hard at the creature. "I know that thing," he says.

Get out of there, now! orders the Dark Man urgently. Run! Get away!

As she backs away, Lexi scoops up two handfuls of snow and rubs them in her eyes. Then she blinks and stares at the fight. The creature is losing ground now. The swarm is attacking! Twin dust tentacles wrap around the dark animal, and it staggers. Its howls clearly communicate pain as well as rage.

"It's falling!" cries Lexi. "It's hurt!"

Run! orders the Dark Man. Get away!

Lexi stops backing away. The tears in her eyes are no longer caused by dust, but by the creature's plight. Its shrieks now sound desperate, confused. In a frenzy, it swings its powerful forelegs with little effect as the swarm flows over them.

Lexi looks desperately up at Jake. "It's dying!"

Get out of there, dang it! shouts Cyril over the link.

Jake puts an arm around Lexi. It is another one of those Jake Bixby moments, where dozens, even hundreds of thoughts and feelings and concerns all click into place in a single second, and he knows exactly what to do.

"Lexi's right," he says into his Spy Link mouthpiece. "We can't just abandon it."

Suddenly a third voice—a very familiar one—breaks into the Spy Link channel.

Okay, children, it says. We got something that might help.

"Marco!" Lexi cries, smiling through tears.

Where are you calling from? demands the Dark Man.

Your lab, replies Marco angrily. Where's the cavalry? Why aren't you helping them?

We'll be there in moments, answers the Dark Man.

Trust me, we're moving with all possible speed.

Kids, listen up, says Marco quickly. **Scoop handfuls of snow and toss them into the air, right into the swarm. Keep doing it. Don't stop. Do you understand? Do not stop.**

Jake turns to Lucas. "Ready?" he asks.

Lucas nods. "It's the Slorg, isn't it?"

"Yes."

"Let's go."

The Bixby brothers scoop up handfuls of snow and advance on the enemy.

That's right, the Slorg.

Most of you Spy Gear kids knew that already, didn't you?

The mysterious dark animal is indeed the Slorg, a genetic hybrid mammal created by Viper and introduced back in Book 2: *The Massively Multiplayer Mystery*. Well, hey, it's back. Actually, it never went away. It's been following the kids through Stoneship Woods for weeks. Whenever Team Spy Gear treks into its HQ, the Slorg quietly follows.

But please don't tell them I told you this.

Cyril, in particular, might collapse into chunks of quivering meat if he knew.

And here's the deal on snow-tossing:

Carrolton's temperature hasn't climbed above twenty-two degrees Fahrenheit since early January. So the snow is quite powdery under the thin, icy surface crust. Thus, as the Bixbys and Lexi hurl handfuls of snow into the sky, each toss explodes into dusty whiteness.

The fluttering flakes drift into the black nanite swarm and get sucked into its whirlwind.

And the swarm reacts.

It stops its assault on the writhing black animal. It stops swirling, too.

Slowly, the swarm gathers into the same billowy, black, smokelike form it used to infiltrate the Stoneship control room. Its sound changes from a dull low-frequency throb to more of a windy hiss.

What's happening? asks Marco.

"I think it's confused," Jake grunts as he heaves two more handfuls of snow.

Keep throwing snow! commands Marco. **You want a constant cloud of ice particles floating through the entity.**

"Oh, we're *throwing*, baby," shouts Lucas. He hurls another handful of powder into the black smoke. "You want a piece of me, fog boy?" He tosses handful after handful. "How about a little of *this*? And some of *this*? And *this*?"

The hissing black cloud drifts back, withdrawing.

Meanwhile, Lexi shovels scoops of powder up into the air just above the rasping black animal that now slumps on the ground.

"Lexi, your snow isn't reaching the swarm," calls Jake as he tosses another snow grenade.

"I'm protecting *him*," she says fiercely, pointing at the creature.

Jake has to smile at her tenacity.

And at that moment, a new sound spreads through the forest: a low, rhythmic thrumming. Seconds later, the trees and bushes start rocking as a downdraft of air rushes in all around.

Lucas points up at the sky.

"Black helicopter!" he shouts.

Sure enough, the sleek, buglike stealth craft hovers directly overhead. Its rotors beat quietly, like a loud whisper. The chopper centers itself over the black fog of the swarm. Then a long tube drops from an open hatch on its underside.

The agitated nanoswarm now looks like a black, boiling fluid. As the helicopter's tube drops into its chaotic midst, the entity sends out tendrils of smoke. These whirl around the tube, as if probing.

Then a loud, roaring suction begins.

"Wow!" shouts Lucas. "It's a big vacuum cleaner!"

The swarm-smoke begins disappearing, sucked violently into the end of the tube. Several small whirlwinds break off from the central entity and flee into the woods. But the bulk of the black swarm is suctioned quickly up the tube to the helicopter.

Greetings from the cavalry, says a strange voice over everyone's Spy Link. **Hotel Quebec and all ground units, this is Charlie One. Contact and collection is complete. Awaiting further orders, over.**

Listening to this exchange, Lucas's face goes rapt with delight. But then he notices Jake and Lexi taking tentative steps toward the black animal, now sprawled in the snow. The creature's breath is loud and labored. It appears to be unconscious.

Charlie One, this is Hotel Quebec, answers the Dark Man gruffly over the channel. **Bring the package home. Over and—**

Lucas quickly cuts in: "Breaker there, Hotel Quebec, sorry, this is . . . uh, Lima Bravo. Please be advised that we also have a package on the ground." He glances up at the hovering helicopter. "Over?"

Roger that, Lima Bravo, says Charlie One.

A bright, greenish halogen spotlight bursts from the underbelly of the craft. Seconds later, it illuminates the fallen creature.

(12)

BIG BOSS LEVEL

6:47 p.m. Agincourt Drive. Two hours later, near Loch Ness Elementary School.

Lucas Bixby sits in the backseat of an idling Mazda. The silver car is old and beat-up, but it runs well and the heater is warm. It idles on the street near the Loch Ness parking lot.

Lucas holds his cell phone to his ear.

"Yes, Mom," he says, wincing.

In the front passenger seat, Jake Bixby raises a pair of Spy Night Vision goggles to his eyes. He trains these on the spillway where Blackwater Creek exits the Enclave, just down the street.

"Looks good," he whispers to Lucas.

"Well, anyway, thanks for holding dinner for us," says Lucas in a flat tone. "Yes, this final strategy session is crucial. The match tomorrow is very, very important, just as I said"—he glances at his watch—"oh, about ninety-six minutes ago."

Now Jake spots two dark figures, one very large and one very small, climbing the embankment from the Enclave spillway. The two jog through the frigid night across the street toward the car.

"Here they come," Jake says quietly.

"Okay, Mom, gotta go now," says Lucas into the phone. "See, like, the entire broomball team is pretty much sitting there, waiting for me. All of them. Waiting. Aging." He covers the mouthpiece, rolls his eyes up to the ceiling, and adds, "Going, criminally, insane."

Outside, the two dark figures split up as they reach the car. Marco hops into the driver's seat; Lexi dives into the backseat next to Lucas. With an exhilarated grin, she gives Lucas a thumbs-up sign.

"Yes! Okay!" says Lucas into the phone. "Right, love you, too. Agreed, excellence *is* its own reward. Will do. Thanks. Bye, Mom."

He flips the phone shut and turns to Lexi, letting out a big sigh.

"Wow," he says.

"It's all good," says Lexi. They slap hands.

"Okay, cool," says Lucas. He reaches into his backpack and pulls out the Spy Video Car headset and joystick remote control unit.

"Calling Delta Leader," Jake says. "Can we get a report on the estate entrance? Over."

All four Mazda occupants wear Spy Link headsets and thus everyone hears the deep, rattling, robotic voice over the channel:

As expected, we have activity here.

The Spy Video Car—let's call him Fred—moves slowly up Blackwater Creek.

Sure, it's dark out . . . especially down here on the creek's icy skin. But Fred sports a nifty infrared light. This light illuminates the area for the car's videocam, yet remains invisible to the human eye.

So Fred moves in the darkness with perfect stealth.

What a guy, that Fred.

Meanwhile, Lucas feels as if he's waited his whole life for this moment. With a contented smile, he adjusts the video screen over his eye.

"Okay, Driver here," he says. "I'm about thirty yards from Tango House. Clean progress. Checking my six before I proceed."

The Spy Video Car travels easily up the creek. Lucas pushes a joystick hard left, turning the car in a tight circle as he scans the video feed carefully.

"Looks all clear," he reports. "Okay, all units, Driver is taking in the UGV."

Be advised of increased security presence, reports a voice with professional calm. **Multiple sentries. Lots of activity.**

Roger that, crackles another voice. **Driver, this is Mothership Alpha. Charlie One reports convoy incoming, unknown designation. We have field teams Alpha, Delta, and Foxtrot moving to waypoint intercept, over.**

"Copy that," says Lucas. "Will proceed with caution, over."

Lexi covers the mouthpiece on her Spy Link headset, then leans forward and taps Marco on the shoulder.

"What the dog is going on?" she asks.

Marco cracks a thin smile. "Aren't you listening?" he asks, covering his mouthpiece, too.

"Yes," whispers Lexi innocently.

Marco nods. "Mothership Alpha is the Agency's mobile command center. Basically, it's like Stoneship HQ stuffed into a big van."

Jake turns to Marco. "Wow! That's awesome."

"The Agency doesn't lack for resources," says Marco.

"What's the other stuff mean?" asks Lexi.

Lucas, grinning as he steers, whispers, "UGV means 'unmanned ground vehicle.'" He thumbs the joysticks with quick precision. "That would be me."

Marco says, "And it sounds like a suspicious-looking convoy of cars is approaching the estate. Three Agency field teams are moving to intercept." He revs the Mazda motor a couple of times. "Should be fun," he adds. "Let's get out of here."

"Why?" asks Jake.

"Multiple security guards are already patrolling Blackwater House," Marco explains. "Now we have vehicles incoming. And kids, I can tell you right now that the Agency is here big-time, with some serious force multipliers in the field. Things could get ugly, fast." Marco fastens his seat belt. "So buckle up, children. Get ready to scoot."

Fred the car swerves around a boulder jutting up through the creek ice. Then he moves quietly under the stone arch of Blackwater House.

The streambed is wide here, almost twenty feet across, and the embankment is high and elaborately landscaped. This serves two purposes: It looks nice, plus it serves as a flood control channel for swollen creek waters during the spring melt.

Up ahead, Fred "sees" two sentries in hooded all-weather gear.

Both stand motionless, like bleak gargoyles, on a raised cobblestone patio built under the archway, no doubt for shady creekside picnics during summertime. A large glass door is recessed into the archway just behind the sentries. Next to the door is a large access panel with a keypad and display screen.

"I hate this part," says one sentry.

The other nods his hood. "The monotony," he says. "The endless waiting."

The first man looks upstream. "Actually, I was referring to the barbecue smell."

The other says, "What barbecue smell?"

"Can't you smell that?" asks the first one.

The other sniffs a few times. "I don't smell a thing."

"Really?" says the first one. He sniffs the sleeve of his gray all-weather poncho. "Maybe I spilled something on myself at dinner last night."

"Hmmm," says the other sentry. "Actually, now that you mention it, I do smell something."

"Is it a barbecue smell?"

The other sentry sniffs loudly for a few seconds. He turns his hooded head from side to side.

Finally he says, "No."

"What is it, then?"

"It's more like a paint smell."

"Maybe somebody barbecued with paint."

The two grim sentries start laughing like idiots.

Wow. Let's pull back really far from these men.

Fortunately, Fred could not "hear" any of this exchange because he is not wired for sound. However, Fred does "see" the red emergency light that starts flashing on the wall just behind the sentries.

* * *

Lucas stares intently at the unfolding scene in the live video feed.

"Something's going on," he says. "The guards just got agitated."

A new voice crackles over the Spy Link: Sir, we have convoy vehicles going evasive. Over!

All units go to Code Red! barks the Dark Man.

Marco sits up. "They're making their move," he says.

Jake cranks down his window and sticks his head out to listen. "Yes, I hear the helicopters," he says, twisting to look upward.

Charlie Two, Charlie Two! calls the first voice. Can we get a light on that intersection? Over.

Repeat, says the Dark Man. All units to Code Red operational positions!

More chatter starts flying over the channel. Two black sedans suddenly roar down Agincourt past the Mazda and speed around the curve. Then a bright halogen spotlight bursts with blinding radiance from the sky, targeting the estate grounds.

Report, Driver! demands the Dark Man. Tell me exactly what's happening, over.

Lucas says, "Roger, uh, the creek-level sentries are punching a code into a keypad panel on the wall. I'm zooming in now, over."

Can you read the display? Over, asks the Dark Man.

"Yes, barely," says Lucas, squinting. "It looks like one, three . . . nine . . . four, five."

Excellent! says the Dark Man.

Marco cuts in. "The access code is likely the same for all entry points in the estate," he says.

Yes, most likely correct, the Dark Man agrees. **Perhaps we can avoid a conspicuous forced entry at the main gate.**

"And save precious search seconds as well," adds Marco.

Lexi whacks him on the shoulder. "How do you know all this stuff?" she asks.

Marco slides the gearshift into first gear. "I'm a wizard-level hacker," he says. "I know everything."

Jake grins and says, "Especially about security measures."

"You got it," says Marco.

"The two sentries just entered the house," Lucas reports, eyeing his video feed.

Marco eases his Mazda forward and noses the car just around the Agincourt bend. Down the street, a big black van and at least six black sedans cluster around the main gate to Blackwater Estate.

Agents pour out of the cars.

"Wow!" says Jake.

"Serious stuff," Marco says.

Main gate open, reports a voice over the Spy Link channel. **We're in.**

Marco grins. "The code worked," he tells Lucas. "Well done, Driver."

But keep doing your job, barks the Dark Man over the link. **We need your eyes on the creek.**

Down the road from the Mazda, agents disappear through the gate, followed by the black sedans. There is a brief pause, then: **Nothing so far. No resistance.**

Meanwhile, Lucas jogs the Spy Video Car backward a few feet to get a wider view under the archway. He grins, honored to bear such a responsibility—the operation's inside eye! He veers left to look upstream. Bright light illuminates the creek on the far side of the arch; this view dims as the spotlight swings away, moving across the estate grounds.

Then Lucas sees the archway door burst open.

"Here they come!" he calls.

First, the two hooded sentries rush out onto the cobblestone patio. Then an indistinct, fuzzy form drifts through the doorway. For a second, it hovers on the patio. Then it suddenly gathers into a shape.

Lucas opens his eyes wide. "It's . . . Old Dan!" he exclaims. He turns to look at Lexi with his uncovered eye. "He's a swarm!"

Roger that, Driver, calls an urgent voice. **Team Bravo, let's get vacuum collection units down into that streambed, now!**

"It must have 'learned' Old Dan months ago, before he died," says Marco.

"What do you mean, learned?" Jake asks.

"Clearly this particular swarm has the ability to log and mimic forms, like the smoke we saw," explains Marco. "And life-forms too. Birds, dogs, whatever . . . and one blind old dude."

Lucas watches Old Dan spin and disperse back into a misty swirl. The whirlwind moves up the creek, following the two sentries.

And then another figure appears in the doorway: a tall, stooped specter in a hooded cloak. The hooded head turns side to side—calmly surveying the creek. Clearly, in no hurry.

"Driver here," reports Lucas, hushed. "I've marked someone else, creekside entrance."

Another swarm entity? the Dark Man asks. **A guard? Please be specific.**

"Neither," answers Lucas.

Of course, Lucas has no way of knowing this for certain. But something about the figure's demeanor is different, almost mesmerizing. His body is so stooped it looks bent over double, yet it glides easily through the doorway. Two large arms push forward eerily beneath the light-colored cloak.

"All I can say is," Lucas goes on, "he looks like, you know . . . the boss."

In the front seat, Marco and Jake exchange a look, eyebrows raised.

Lucas leans forward, as if this could afford him a closer

view. He watches the tall figure emerge from the door-way onto the patio. But the gray cloak still drapes backward through the doorway, extending straight back from his waist.

"What the flying monkey is he?" asks Lucas.

But suddenly the video heads-up display goes awash in white.

"I've lost picture!" Lucas yells. "The spotlight! It's hitting the camera!"

Charlie One, move the light! shouts the Dark Man.

Other voices cut into the channel. For a few seconds, chaos reigns. But finally the brightness dims. The washed-out screen static dissipates. And when Lucas can see into the archway again, the patio is deserted.

"They're gone!" he shouts. "Hotel Quebec, all units, they're gone." He quickly swings the spy car in a circle. "No sign of them anywhere."

Jake hangs out the window again. He feels the whispery thrum of the Agency helicopter as it passes overhead. Then he sees its spotlight swing suddenly to train down into the estate.

All units, we've got a flyer! shouts a voice. **Repeat, we've got—**

The transmission cuts off in midsentence. Jake watches the helicopter bob and dip sharply to the right. Then he hears a familiar sound: the powerful whine of a jet engine, but quieter. And he sees, rising above the

Enclave wall, rising slowly above the rocking trees, the circular craft with multicolored lights ringing the bottom edge.

"Viper's hovercraft!" he cries, pointing.

Marco and the kids scramble out of the car onto the street and look up.

The craft hovers motionless above Blackwater House.

"Get him!" shouts Lexi.

Off to the south, Jake sees the black helicopter bank hard into what looks like an attack run, flying directly at the airship. For a brief moment it appears the two aircraft will collide.

But then the colored lights of the airship start to spin. The craft rises vertically with lightning speed as the helicopter whizzes past beneath it. Then, with a hissing metallic whine, the hovercraft tilts slightly and accelerates—faster than any helicopter could *possibly* travel.

It is gone before Jake can say, "It's gone."

And in just a blink it is over the horizon.

13

THE PERFECT ENDING

Saturday, February 2. 9:27 a.m. Cyril cringes at the bone-crunching sound. "Can Brill actually *do* that with his stick?" he asks.

Beside him on the bench, the man in the hockey mask is silent.

"Get up, Lexi!" shouts Cyril. "Come on, kid! It's not like it's *completely* broken!"

Out on the Bald Spot ice, the game is wild and woolly. The Wolf Pack is hitting hard, and it's clear that Brill, Wilson, and crew are out for blood. Every body check is brutal; every stick slash is vicious. The wolves clearly want to start a fist fight, too. But every time a confrontation arises, all Wolf Pack eyes turn to the Team Spy Gear bench.

There Cyril sits wrapped like a mummy in blankets,

his Siberian sheepskin tundra hat with fur earflaps pulled low, clopping his huge mittens together as he cheers hoarsely for the team. His recovery from illness keeps him from the lineup today.

But that's not what the wolves are looking at.

Next to Cyril sits a very large man wearing a hockey mask painted like a skull. He also holds a ceremonial Masai spear.

"Marco," Cyril asks, "why does everybody keep looking at me?" He points out at the ice. "Look, they're doing it again!"

"They fear you," says Marco.

"You think so?" asks Cyril. He glances over at the Wolf Pack bench, where a few subs sit watching the action. "Hey, dog boys!" he calls happily.

The Wolf Pack subs give Cyril a hateful glance. Behind Cyril, Marco stands up, jams his spear deeper into the snow, and leans on it. He opens his eyes wide, then sticks his tongue out through his hockey mask's narrow mouth hole and waggles it.

The Wolf faces turn white with fear.

Cyril grins, nodding. "You're right," he says. "Somehow, I frighten them now." Then he frowns. "The question is, why?" He thinks a moment. "It could be my hair."

"It's your face," says Marco, sitting back down.

Cyril nods. "Yes, you're right. It's my face." He frowns again. "But why?"

"Something grim and pitiless in your eyes, no doubt," Marco says.

Cyril looks at Marco. "Yes, that's plausible."

"Could be illness-related," says Marco.

Cyril nods thoughtfully. Then he says, "Yes, perhaps the flu has changed me. Made me more dangerous and intimidating."

"I suppose we could ponder this all day," says Marco.

"That would be fun," says Cyril. He pulls a stopwatch out of his coat pocket. "Whoa, it's almost halftime. Chuck me that horn, will you?"

Marco plucks Mr. Latimer's air horn from a snow pile near his end of the bench and tosses it to Cyril. Cyril clasps the trigger and stares at the stopwatch, counting down silently. Then he blasts the horn.

"That's half!" he shouts. "Off the ice! Let's stem the bleeding, folks!"

The Bixbys, Lexi, their goalkeeper Justin Bolby, and two mystery kids in ski masks tromp off the ice, all gasping. One mystery kid walks several yards past the bench, collapses in the snow, and shrieks, "We *suck! Raccoons* could beat us!" This is Norris Fletcher, the team's center; he's extremely competitive.

Justin Bolby drops next to Norris, curls into a ball, and says, "I see only the void."

"Oh, you actually *see* something?" growls Norris. "Your performance in goal would make a matador proud."

The other mystery kid joins the Bixbys and Lexi at the team bench. She whips off a ski mask to reveal herself as Cat Horton. She's taking Cyril's spot today. In shock, she collapses on the bench next to him.

"This is a *very* bad experience," she says. "This is not good for me. Really, this needs to end. Is there an end in sight?"

"Cat, you're doing *great*," says Cyril, patting her on the back. "Except for all those times you kept falling down, like, every second and stuff, and the crying. Girl, that's gotta stop."

"I wasn't *crying*," says Cat. "It was more like whimper-ing."

"We're losing really bad," Lexi says, tossing down her broomball stick in anger.

"Hey, it's only six to three," Lucas gasps. "It just *seems* bad because they're knocking the holy living cornstalks out of us."

"It's a physical match," agrees Jake, who has a bloody wad of Kleenex stuffed up one nostril.

"Physical?" yells Lucas. "Brill held me at gunpoint dur-ing that last power play. And did you see Wilson's broomball stick? *He has human skulls hanging from it!*"

Cyril slams a fist into his palm. "I say it's time we fix bayonets."

Lexi looks over at Marco. "That's a really scary mask," she says.

"Thanks, Tinkerbell."

"Why are you wearing it?" she asks.

"It's warm," says Marco.

Lexi nods. "What's up with the spear?"

Marco looks at his Masai spear. "Well, it's always brought me good luck," he says. "But the way you guys are playing . . ." He pauses, gazing out at the ice. "The spear won't help."

"I'm sure it's too *embarrassed* to help," says Cyril.

Jake whaps Marco on the shoulder. "I didn't see you arrive, man," he says.

Marco whips off the mask. "I have news," he says.

Jake glances over at Justin and Norris, who whine at each other several yards away. Then he looks at Cat. Cat gives him a dark glare.

"Hey, I think I'll go make a *snow cone!*" she says. She gets up and walks away.

Jake grins. "I like her," he says to Cyril.

"She's adequate," says Cyril.

Marco stands up and gestures to the bench. "Sit down, people," he says. "You look tired."

Jake, Lucas, and Lexi plop onto the bench.

Marco says, "Okay, so I've been hanging out at the Agency lab and some very—"

"What about the Slorg?" interrupts Lexi.

"Still under observation," Marco replies. "They have it sedated in an oxygen chamber." He notes Lexi's concern and adds, "Its lungs were damaged, but the biology team thinks the prognosis is good."

"Okay," says Lexi.

"So what kind of animal is it?" Lucas asks.

"Tissue samples are still being analyzed," says Marco with amusement. "That's the official answer."

"And the unofficial answer?" asks Lucas.

"It's a Slorg."

Lucas grins. He pulls off his helmet and says, "I hope the Agency has a world-class geneticist."

"If they don't," says Marco, "I'm sure they'll abduct one soon."

Lexi looks up at Marco. "He saved us from the swarm," she says.

"I know," says Marco.

"Tell them that."

Marco stares at her for a second. "Yes, I'll *remind* them." He raises his craggy brow. "Actually, the bioteam did learn something . . . unexpected." He grins at Cyril. "The Slorg is an herbivore."

"What!" Cyril laughs.

"Yeah, it hates meat," says Marco.

"That makes sense, when you think about it," says Lucas. "Why would Viper bioengineer a breed that could, like, eat him?"

Jake tears off his gloves and says, "So what did they find inside Blackwater House?"

Marco wraps both hands around his spear.

"Just what you'd expect," he says. "A ridiculously sophisticated and expensive nanofabrication lab. Holding chambers for nanite swarms. Molecular-level control systems . . . the works. Very advanced stuff. So advanced, it almost boggles the mind." Marco shakes his head. "And all of it was *totally* fried. Just like the quantum computer lab you guys found in December. They triggered a hot self-destruct that toasted everything, including all of the command-and-control software."

"So Intelligent NanoSystems with its fake Lakeshore address was just a front for Viper's secret lab," says Jake.

"Right," Marco says. "He needed a cover for all the suspicious shipments, coming and going."

"What about the snow devils that escaped from the helicopter's vacuum?" asks Jake. "We saw them spin off into Stoneship Woods."

"Dormant, most likely," says Marco. "Shut down. Agency techs are pretty sure that although Viper's swarms are programmed to evolve and mimic, they require an activation signal from a central transmitter. There was such a transmitter at the Blackwater lab . . . and it was fried to a crisp."

Lucas folds his arms. "So where does Viper get all this amazing stuff?"

"The Agency is *very* concerned about that," says Marco. "Look, Viper's technology applications continue to surpass—and I mean *easily* surpass—the work produced by the biggest and best-funded research laboratories in the world, whether government, university, or private. He's got an input stream of money and knowledge from somewhere that keeps him a full step ahead of the leading edge in human applied science."

"That's kind of spooky," says Jake.

"Yes, it is," Marco replies. "Hey, you saw his airship. Not even the most advanced aircraft prototype in the world can do what that craft did last night."

Everybody stares into space for a while as this sinks in. Then Lucas clears his throat.

"So was that . . . Viper I saw?" he asks. "Under the arch?"

Marco shrugs. "Nobody can know," he says.

"It gives me chills," says Lexi.

"Yeah, it gives *him* chills too." Marco nods across Ridgeview Drive toward the tree line of Stoneship Woods. There a huge dark figure leans on a tree, watching.

"Why is *he* here?" asks Cyril.

"He loves sports," says Marco.

"Ha!" Cyril barks. "I'm sure he's got fifty bucks on the Wolf Pack right now."

"Get used to seeing him around," says Marco. He looks at Lucas. "Your possible Viper sighting has everyone on edge."

"If it *is* Viper, why does he keep coming here?" asks Lexi.

"Good question," Marco says. "Carrolton seems to be ground zero for his evil plans, doesn't it?" He pulls the hockey mask back over his face. "Say, don't you jokers have another period to play?"

"Wait," says Jake. "One last question."

"Okay. But make it short. I want to sink back into brooding menace."

"The Omega Link," says Jake. "It sent us those messages, 'nanite' and 'ecophagy.' So somebody obviously knew what Viper was doing."

"Sort of," Marco says. "The Agency managed to collect an actual nanite sample last week. That swarm was indeed self-replicating and displayed some crude intelligence . . . but it turned out to be a booby trap."

"How so?" asks Jake.

"It was designed to transport the respiratory illness the Dark Man told you about," Marco explains. "A lung infection that knocked the Agency off its feet for a while." Marco hefts the Masai spear in his hands. "So Dark Man and company knew nanites were on the prowl, and he feared the worst—a doomsday dust scenario, with Viper armed and ready to pull the nano-trigger. But he had no idea where the research and development lab might be located. None whatsoever."

Lucas smiles. "But then Old Dan led us to Blackwater House."

"Right," agrees Marco. "And thus it was your work,

once again, that led the Agency to Viper's lab."

"Heroes again," says Cyril to Jake.

Jake grins and says, "Dog."

"Dog," replies Cyril. They punch fists.

Then Cyril checks his stopwatch again. "Oops," he says. "Time's up." He raises the air horn and gives it a quick blast.

Lucas turns to Jake, who is the team captain. "What kind of tactical adjustments should we make in the second period?" he asks.

Jake says, "Let's play better."

"Okay!" everybody cries at once.

And as Team Spy Gear clacks their sticks together and then heads out onto the ice, the satellite camera view starts to pull away. Hey, wait a minute! Not yet! We want to watch the second period!

But it's too late. Once the zoom-out begins, there's no stopping it.

Already the ice rink is shrinking. Down below, the opening face-off of Period Two looks like ants squabbling over a tiny crumb of coffee cake. Whoa! Now one particularly small ant with long black ant-hair streaks up the right wing with the crumb.

It shoots! It scores! Ants go nuts.

And back farther we zoom. Everything looks so white and clean, doesn't it?

Floating up here like a big squid eye in the sky, gazing

down on Carrolton's frozen tundra, it's easy to get philosophical about things. Life doesn't always give us perfect endings, so guys who write books often try to make up perfect endings so everybody feels better.

But not me. I report the facts. Otherwise I'd be just a lowly novelist.

So when I tell you that a Wave of Goodness suddenly washes over Carrolton below—over the reservoir, the mall, the houses and school yards, the business district— you can trust that I'm telling you the truth. Oh sure, pockets of darkness and slimy intentions still pool up in hidden corners. As a seasoned reporter, I won't sugarcoat that fact. Something hooded and evil and alien still lurks down there.

But right now, overall . . . things are looking good.

Kids, let's enjoy it while we can. Oh, and some big news just came in.

Please go to the next page.

BIG WIN FOR TEAM SPY GEAR!

Lopez Hat Trick Spearheads Victory

CARROLTON (Reuters)—Fueled by a relentless second-period assault led by high-scoring wing Lexi Lopez and capped by a stunning last-second goal from newcomer Cat Horton, Team Spy Gear successfully defended its home ice with a stirring 9–8 comeback victory over the Wolf Pack at the Bald Spot today.

"It's a great, great victory for all of us," said interim coach Cyril Wong after the contest. "Especially me."

Down 6–3 after the first period, TSG regrouped by making brilliant tactical adjustments during the halftime break. When asked about his halftime instructions to the team, Coach Wong replied, "Did you know that a Siberian tiger can eat sixty pounds of meat at one feeding? I find that somewhat sickening."

Lopez, TSG's star right wing, came out blazing after the break. Shut down by aggressive Wolf Pack defenders in the first period, Lopez broke loose in Period Two, knocking home three goals in the first eight minutes. Two of those scores came after nifty stick-handling moves that put the ball through a large ugly defender's legs.

"I'm good," said Lopez.

Wolf Pack ugly defender and team captain Brill Joseph

pointed to Team Spy Gear's superior bench strength as the key factor in his team's collapse.

"If not for that guy on their bench, we would have beaten them into [censored] marmalade," he said.

The game-winning goal itself was a stunner. A late Wilson Wills deflection past TSG goalie Justin Bolby (who logged zero saves in the contest—all eight Wolf shots on goal went in) had just brought the Wolf Pack back even at 8–8. But moments later a wild frenzy in front of the Wolves' net ended in a dramatic backhand shot by Horton, playing her first game in a TSG uniform.

Sprawled on the ice with her eyes closed, the rookie left wing had raised her stick just as a Pack defender cleared the ball out of the crease. The ball caught Horton's stick squarely and rebounded hard into the Wolf goal.

"I was trying to surrender," Horton explained. "Mostly I just wanted my mommy."

The shot hit the net just seconds before the final horn sounded, triggering a wild celebration by the TSG side.

"What a superswell team win," exclaimed Team Spy Gear captain Jake Bixby. "Gosh, I'm elated. Golly." Snickers from teammates indicated similar emotions.

Interim Coach Wong agreed. "Normally, I prefer individual glory," he said. "But beating the Wolf Pack is something worth sharing, which is something I haven't done since they forced me to in preschool."

As of yet, no rematch is planned.

Amazing Squid Fact!

Did you know?

Sure, its massive, drool-smeared tusks can puncture a garbage truck, and its tentacles can suck the skin off a cow in just seconds.

But did you know that the giant squid has the *largest eyes* of any known animal? Just one squid eye can be more than *fifteen inches wide*! Amazing but true!

Kids, imagine *that* peeking out from under your bed in the middle of the night!

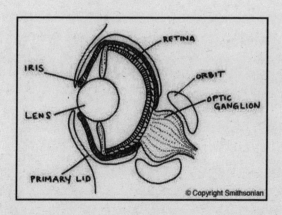

Turn the page for a Sneak Peek at . . .

SPY GEAR ADVENTURES
BOOK 5

THE SHRIEKING SHADOW

1

BUBBLES IN THE LAGOON

Spring has sprung in Carrolton like . . . oh, like a *madman crazed with insanity!* Okay, maybe that's lame. But I can't help it! Life is exploding everywhere! After the frigid lockdown of Carrolton's brutal winter, the sight of green tree buds makes everyone in town go wacky with wackiness.

Just look at them down there.

Oh. Please zoom in your telescopic photo lens to a magnification of 600X.

Okay, now focus in on that big green square covered with white rectangles. That's the Carrolton Soccer Complex. It's big. . . . So big that it's one of only eight hundred suburban soccer complexes that can be seen with the naked eye from the International Space Station.[1]

If you zoom in another 30X or so, you see that these

1. You may recall that my office is located here.

particular soccer fields are covered with ants. Wait! Those are kids, not ants. Sorry.

Yes, it's Saturday in spring, and that means soccer! See the hundreds of kids waving their feelers in the air, clamping their huge jaws around crumbs that look like boulders, and digging in all eight legs as they haul the massive food chunks back to the hive, and ... . Wait a minute. Those actually *are* ants. Apparently, you zoomed in too far. (This seems to happen to us at least once every book, doesn't it?)

But no, wait, these aren't ants. Ants have six legs, not eight. What are these things? Spiders, maybe? Spiders have eight legs, right? But these don't look or act like spiders. Spiders are solitary; they don't swarm like this or live in colonies.

Interesting. Okay, well, let's move on, shall we? This isn't the Discovery Channel, after all.

Zoom out now.

Ah, there we go. Over there, on the grass.

See? *Those* are kids. Soccer kids. Hundreds of them. Thousands, maybe.

Pan your Spy Cam northwest from the Soccer Complex, across Agincourt Drive, across Blackwater Creek, across Agincourt Drive again, then across Agincourt Drive again. See that gray house, the colonial at 44444 Agincourt Drive? That's the Bixby house.

Now peer into the windows and violate their privacy, like a good spy.

Hmmm, nobody's home.

Scan around again. Follow the sidewalks. Slowly.

While you're at it, check out those lawns. Don't they look healthy?

That's because they actually *are* healthy.

See, unlike in other towns, where people nuke their weeds with industrial poisons, folks in Carrolton generally use organic and poison-free methods of gardening and lawn care. I say "generally" because there are exceptions. Every once in a while, some fool tries to lay down a patch of toxic sludge to kill off some poor species of plant that never did anything wrong other than fail to be Kentucky bluegrass.

But then that neighbor gets to meet Dr. Tim.

When I say "meet Dr. Tim," I say it loudly with quotation marks around it.

Because if you're spraying common garden poisons on your lawn anywhere in Dr. Tim's neighborhood, which is the Bixbys' neighborhood too, the way you "meet" Dr. Tim is by running in terror as he chases you with a Bolivian machete.

Uh oh, looks like we're about to get a demonstration.

See that guy over there? That's Ted Barky. He's new in town.

Note how Ted sprays a yellow hissing liquid onto the dandelions by his sidewalk.

Do you hear that? That little squeaking sound? That's the sound of dandelions shrieking in agony.

Note also the product name on Ted's spray bottle: Weedslaughter Plus. How bad is the stuff? This bad: When Ted shakes the bottle, insane laughter can be heard. It comes from inside the bottle.

Note also how neighbors up and down Agincourt Drive stare in utter disbelief at Ted Barky. Some start edging toward their houses. Then a white pickup truck rolls slowly around the corner; the neighbors drop their gardening tools and hurry inside. Doors slam up and down the street.

But poor Ted doesn't notice.

He just keeps spraying the smoking, fizzling, bubbling yellow liquid onto his lawn.

The white pickup truck stops next to Ted, and Dr. Tim steps out. Ted glances up, nods in a neighborly way, and keeps slaying weeds with lethal toxins. Then he suddenly halts the slaughter. He frowns and crouches low, staring at something on the ground.

Dr. Tim approaches.

Dr. Tim has become the neighborhood lawn cop. He angrily patrols the streets, on the lookout for poison usage. People fear him. It doesn't help that Dr. Tim also *looks* insane, with his torn gaucho hat nestled atop huge, bushy white eyebrows. His wild white mustache and piercing blue eyes give people the notion that he's a madman capable of unspeakable mayhem.

"Say," he says loudly. "I'm wondering, Ted, what is that yellow stuff there?"

"Weed killer," says Ted, still staring at the ground.

"Weed killer," repeats Dr. Tim. His smile looks like a grimace of searing pain.

"Yes," says Ted. "I use it to kill my weeds."

"Do you mind if I . . . look at the bottle, Ted?" If you knew Dr. Tim like I do, you'd know that he is struggling right now to keep from sprouting fangs and then sinking them into Ted Barky's throat.

"Why?" asks Ted, glancing up again.

"I want to scan the ingredients," says Dr. Tim. "I'm a scientist, Ted."

"Really?" Ted hands the Weedslaughter Plus spray bottle to Dr. Tim. "Say, Tim, since you're a scientist, do you know anything about ants?"

Dr. Tim takes a deep breath. Then he says, "Ted, I know *everything* about ants."

"Look at these guys," says Ted, pointing at the edge of his lawn. "Check out that anthill."

Dr. Tim crouches and jabs his nose inches from the grass. "Those aren't ants," he says.

"They're not?" says Ted, puzzled. "They look like ants."

Dr. Tim nods. "But ants have six legs," he says. "These have eight."

"Maybe they're spiders," says Ted.

"Spiders don't have three body segments or live in colonies," says Dr. Tim. "These do."

(Say, doesn't this sound familiar?)

"Well, they look like ants," says Ted.

"But they're not," says Dr. Tim. "In fact, these are anything but ants."

"Then what are they?"

"I don't know."

Dr. Tim thrusts his hand into his pants pocket and yanks out a tiny plastic tube with a screened lid. He uncaps the tube, scoops up several of the odd insects—maybe nine or ten of them, plus a bit of their colony structure—and pops the lid back on.

Then he turns and glares deeply into Ted Barky's eyes.

Ted faints.

Grinning, Dr. Tim trudges back to his pickup truck. He doesn't mind scaring people if it means fewer poisons in our environment. As Tim trudges, he glances at the specimen tube. Then he stops.

He frowns, staring at the tube.

Where there had been nearly a dozen antlike insects, now there's only one.

And it's huge.

* * *

Okay, this is getting ridiculous. Where the heck are the Bixbys?

Did Viper abduct them?

Let's keep looking.

Pan down to the Carrolton Reservoir. Check out that sailboat with the big yellow spinnaker sail. See how it glides over the light chop? I love that. Watch how it fills with wind and—

Wait! Did you see that?

Surely you did.

No?

Hmmm. I could have sworn I saw something really big underwater. Are you sure you didn't see that big shadow just under the surface?

It was moving pretty fast.

Okay. Maybe not.

Well, that's the thing about water, especially big water like the Carrolton Reservoir. *Anything* could be swimming in there: sharks, squids, whatever. Well, not in a freshwater lake, of course. I mean, *heh heh*, you wouldn't see scary saltwater ocean creatures in a reservoir, would you? No. Of course not. Something really big or dangerous in a freshwater reservoir would be unusual. Maybe one of a kind. A freak.

Whatever. I don't know why I'm bringing that up.

So anyway, let's pan back over to the Lakeside Green. We finally found the Bixbys.

* * *

The soccer ball rolls to a halt near the chain-link fence that lines the golf course.

Jake Bixby reaches the sphere, nimbly flicks it upward with his toe, and catches it. Then he stares at something nearby.

"What the left donkey's hoof is that?" he asks, pointing onto the municipal course where, a good fifty yards away, one of the taller, spindlier shrubs is floating down the fairway. No wait, that's not a shrub. It's a mop. Actually no, it's not a mop either.

"Hey, that's Cyril!" exclaims Jake.

Lucas steps up next to his brother.

"Who, that guy?" he says. "No way! Look, he's carrying a golf bag."

"Right," agrees Jake. "That couldn't be Cyril."

The hairy golfer stops and pulls a club out of his bag. He drops the bag, seizes the club with both hands, and starts hacking gruesomely at something in the tall grass of the left rough.

"He's killing something," says Lucas suspiciously.

"My god, that's heinous," says Jake.

Now the golfer lifts the club high over his head, pauses, and takes a huge violent swing. The momentum twists his upper body so wildly that his hips lock and his legs buckle. The club's arc continues all the way around in a complete circle. As the club swings upward, the golfer's legs splay out at impossible angles and he collapses into a pile of dislocated limbs.

"You're right," says Lucas. "That *is* Cyril."

Jake grins. "And look who's with him."

A dark-haired girl in glasses slogs up beside Cyril, who thrashes about like a rubbery squid-man on the ground. She carries a golf bag too. The girl gazes down at Cyril for a minute, then reaches down and gives him a hand, yanking him back onto his feet.

"It's Cat!" says Lucas.

Jake grins again—this time mischievously. Hey, a Bixby knows a good opportunity when he sees it. He drops low and scrambles to a bush near the fence.

"Come on, Broseph," he calls back to Lucas, grinning wildly. "Let's spy on them!"

Lucas Bixby immediately "goes electronic" on the situation, something he often does. He whips out a pair of Micro Listeners, tosses one to Jake, and jabs his unit's earpiece into his ear.

Both boys listen in on the conversation. But to make things easier for you, let's move the camera over by Cyril and Cat.

Cyril shades his eyes as he gazes up the fairway toward the tee box.

"Was that a good golf?" he asks Cat. "I didn't see where it went. Did I golf it okay? Was it acceptable golfage?"

"Not quite," replies Cat.

"Why not?" asks Cyril.

"Well, Cyril, you missed the ball," says Cat. "See?" She points at the ground. "There it is."

"That's my golf ball?" asks Cyril. "It looks so *small*."

"Yes," says Cat patiently. "Plus you were hitting back toward the tee, back where we started this hole, oh, about two hours ago."

"I was?"

"Yes," says Cat. She takes a deep breath. "Remember how I told you about hitting toward the flag?" She points down the fairway toward the distant green. "See it way down there?"

Cyril nods, looking. "That's miles away."

Cat drops her own golf bag.

"Let's rest," she says wearily.

Cyril nods his hair vigorously. "I'm exhausted," he says. "It's been a long day." Both kids sit on the fairway grass. "Say, when does golf end? Like, what's our time limit?"

"You just play eighteen holes," says Cat.

Cyril looks horrified. "They make you do this *eighteen times*?" He stands up again. "But what if your timer runs out?"

"There is no timer, Cyril," says Cat. "You keep playing until you're finished." She looks up at the sky. "Or in our case, until darkness falls."

"Dang!" says Cyril, centering his club over the ball again. "Let's golf!"

Cyril takes another insane swing. But this time, miraculously, he makes solid contact. *Thwock!* The tiny white ball rockets in a majestic arc down the fairway. As it flies, it hooks left and sails into a line of trees on the fairway's left edge. After a few sharp cracks, silence.

"Wow," says Cat, watching in awe. "Nice hit. But I hope it isn't in the lagoon."

"What lagoon?"

"The Long Lagoon," says Cat. "It's a man-made lake that curves through four different holes."

"Why would they do that?" asks Cyril. "That's totally monkeys."

Cat shrugs.

"I mean, dude, come on," continues Cyril. "How can you achieve golfness if there's a bunch of water all over the place?"

"Cyril, water hazards are supposed to make shot selection more challenging," explains Cat.

"Why?"

"Because it's . . . more fun," says Cat.

"Why?"

"Let's go," sighs Cat.

The two pick up their bags and trudge, clubs clanking, down the fairway. As they approach the Scotch pines on the left side, a loud splashing noise rises from behind the tree line. At first it sounds like a big lawn sprinkler hissing to life. But then it transforms into a low rumbling that slowly fades away.

"What the Barnaby was that?" asks Cyril.

Cat frowns. "Maybe they're dredging the lagoon for golf balls," she says.

"Cool!" says Cyril. "Let's check it out."

The two reach the trees and start pushing through low pine branches. Just as they reach the moody, tree-darkened lagoon, a foamy jet of water, rising maybe twenty feet high, drops back into the lagoon.

"What's that?" asks Cyril.

"I don't know," Cat answers. "Some kind of fountain, I guess."

"So this is the lost lagoon," intones Cyril.

"The *Long* Lagoon," corrects Cat, looking around. "Let's find your ball and get out of here."

Cyril gazes into the water. "I hope it's not, like, in the drink," he says. "I didn't bring my, uh . . . my . . . scuba stuff."

Cyril stutters through that last statement because he sees a vague shadow gliding underwater around a curve in the shoreline about thirty yards away. It disappears behind a clump of bald cypress trees jutting from the water.

Cyril frowns. "Gee, that's odd," he mumbles to himself.

Suddenly, an ear-splitting shriek explodes from the grove. It is so loud, cypress leaves shudder.

Cyril and Cat freeze.

They hear something hiss and splash behind the cypress trees. Then Cat points out at the murky green water.

"Cyril," she whispers, pointing.

A dark shape, just under the surface, glides around the cypress grove.

It is very large.

As it moves, it pushes a ripple ahead . . . and leaves a bubbly trail of foam behind.

It heads directly toward Cat and Cyril.